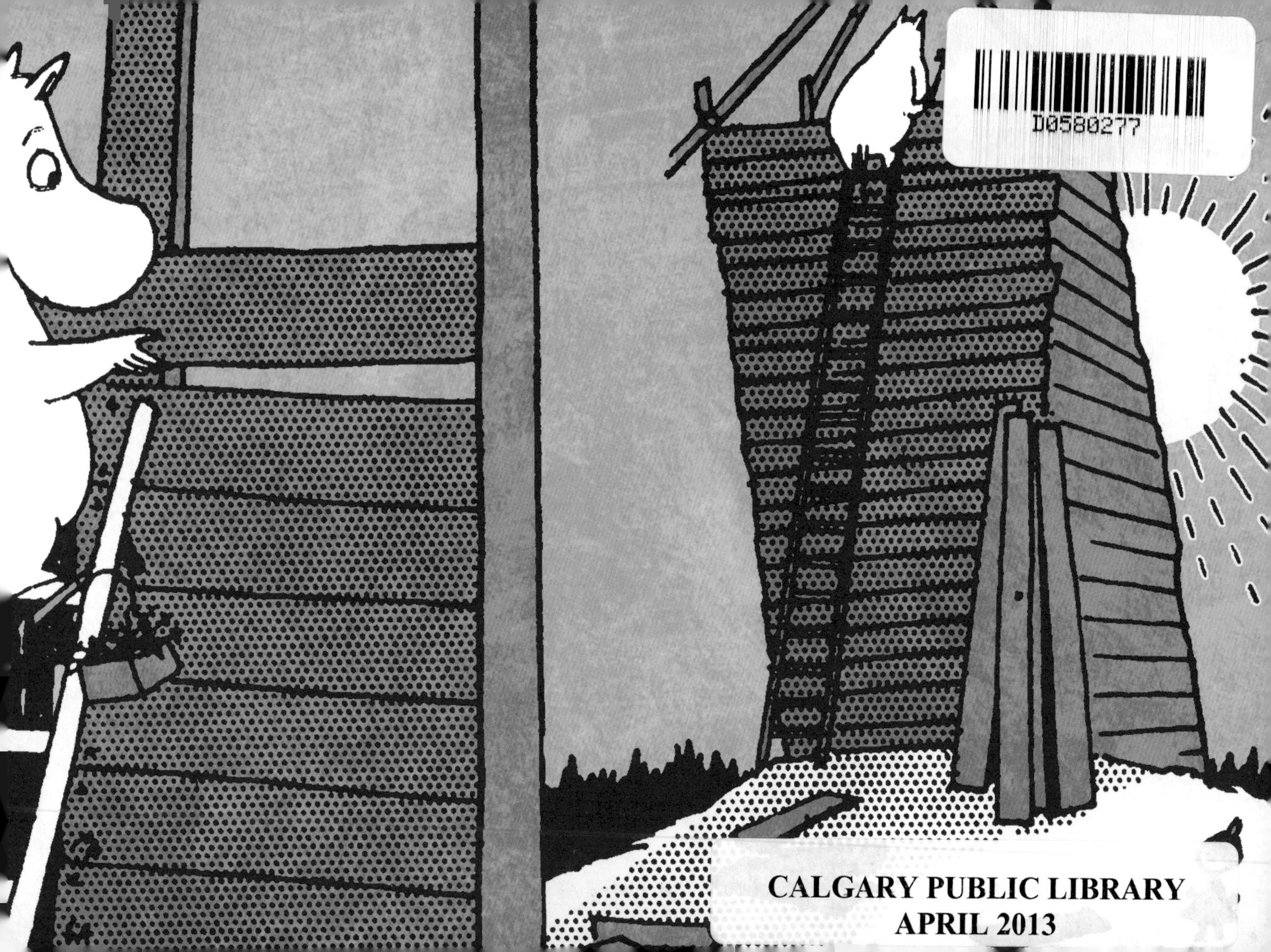

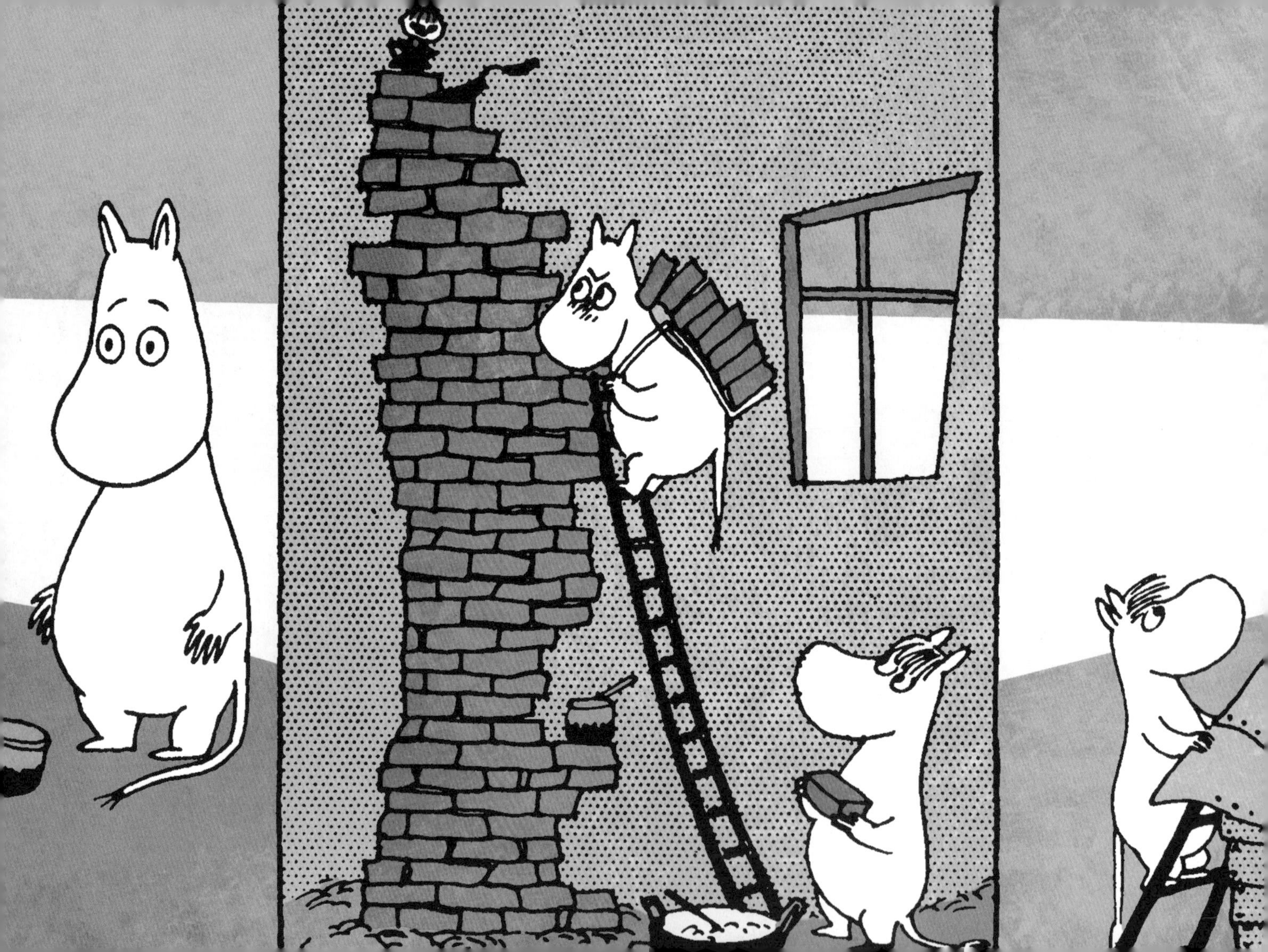

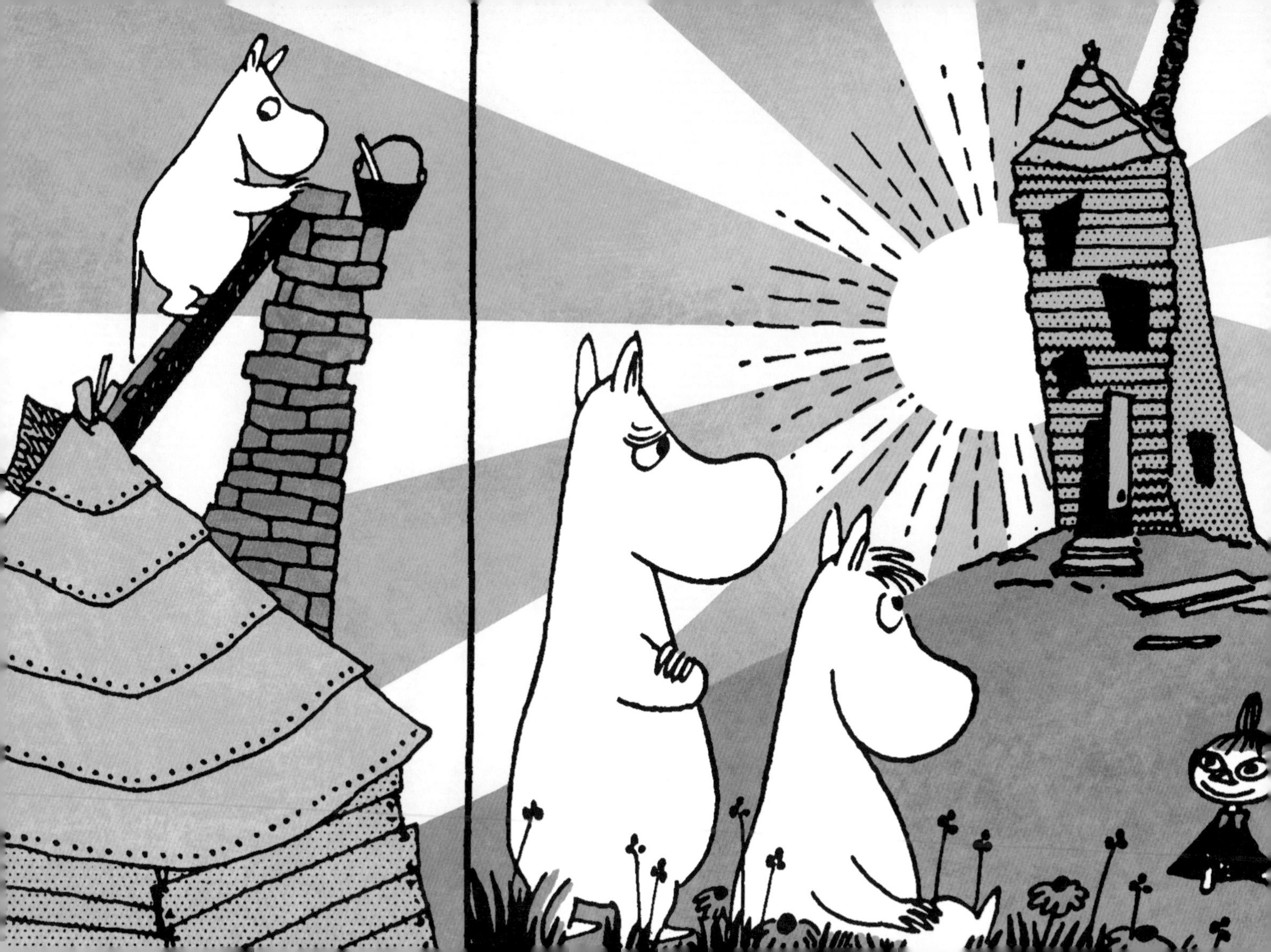

Enfant is an imprint of Drawn & Quarterly.

www.drawnandquarterly.com

First edition: January 2013
Printed in Malaysia
10 9 8 7 6 5 4 3 2 1

Library and Archives Canada Cataloguing in Publication
Jansson, Tove
Moomin Builds a House / Tove Jansson.
ISBN 978-1-77046-108-6
1. Graphic novels. I. Title.
PZ7.7.J35M26 2013 j741.5'94897
C2012-905375-9

Published in the USA by Enfant, a client publisher of
Farrar, Straus and Giroux
18 West 18th Street
New York, NY 10011
Orders: 888.330.8477

Published in Canada by Enfant, a client publisher of
Raincoast Books
2440 Viking Way
Richmond, BC V6V 1N2
Orders: 800.663.5714

Distributed in the United Kingdom by
Publishers Group UK
63-66 Hatton Garden
London
EC1N 8LE
info@pguk.co.uk

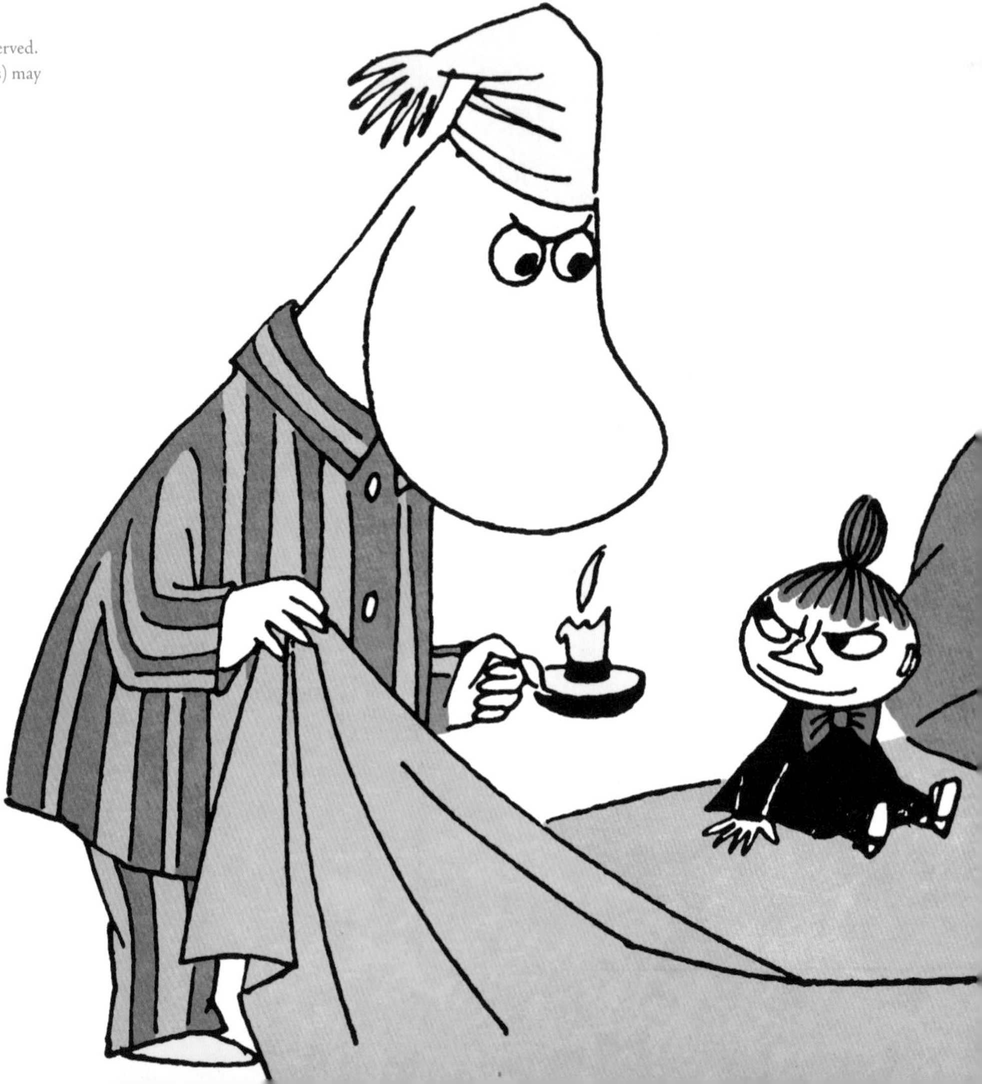

MOOMIN BUILDS A HOUSE

Tove Jansson

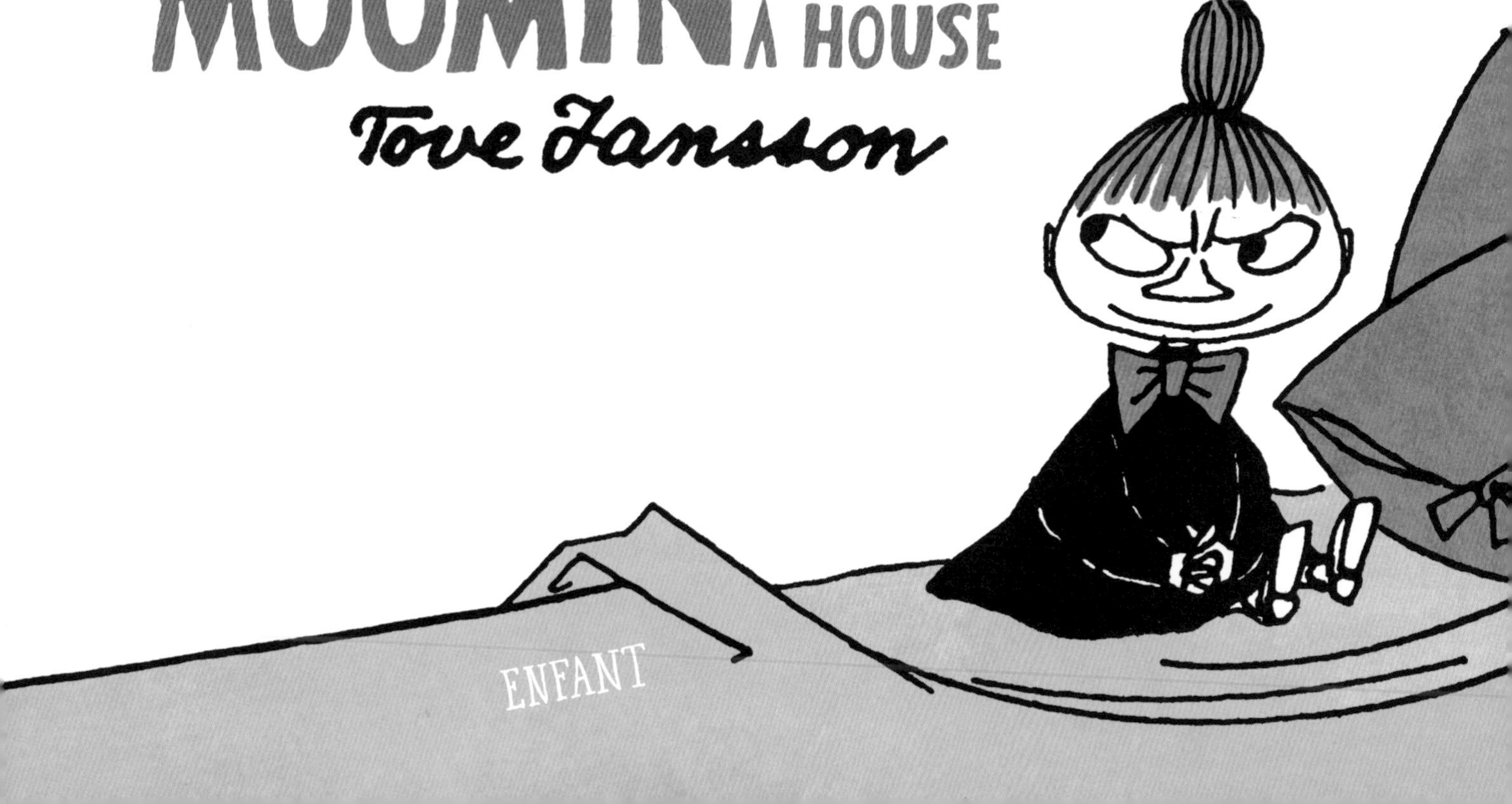

ENFANT

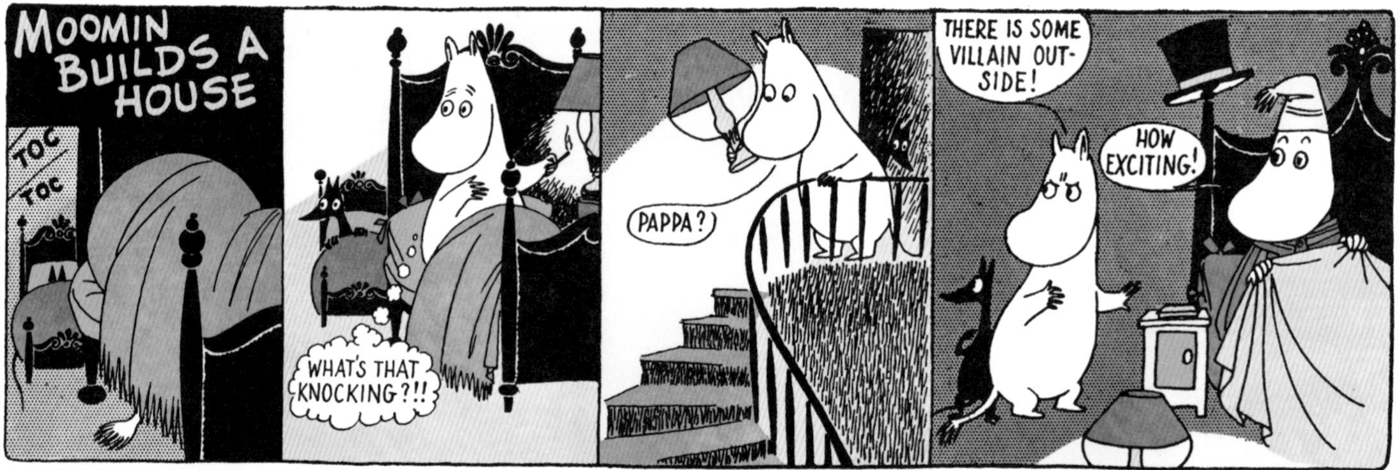
MOOMIN BUILDS A HOUSE
TOC TOC
WHAT'S THAT KNOCKING?!!
PAPPA?
THERE IS SOME VILLAIN OUT-SIDE!
HOW EXCITING!

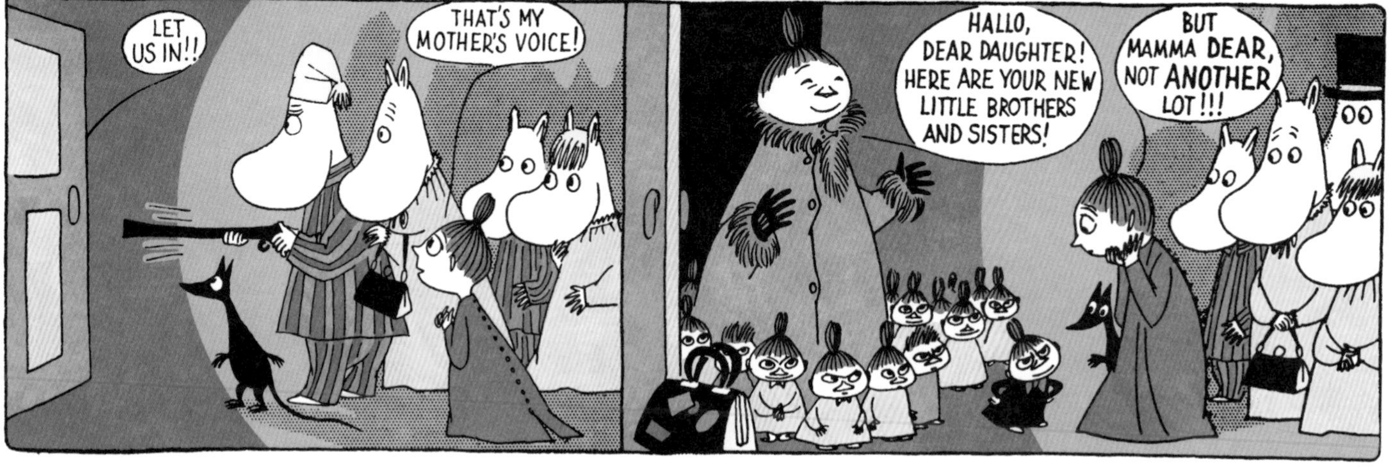
LET US IN!!
THAT'S MY MOTHER'S VOICE!
HALLO, DEAR DAUGHTER! HERE ARE YOUR NEW LITTLE BROTHERS AND SISTERS!
BUT MAMMA DEAR, NOT ANOTHER LOT!!!

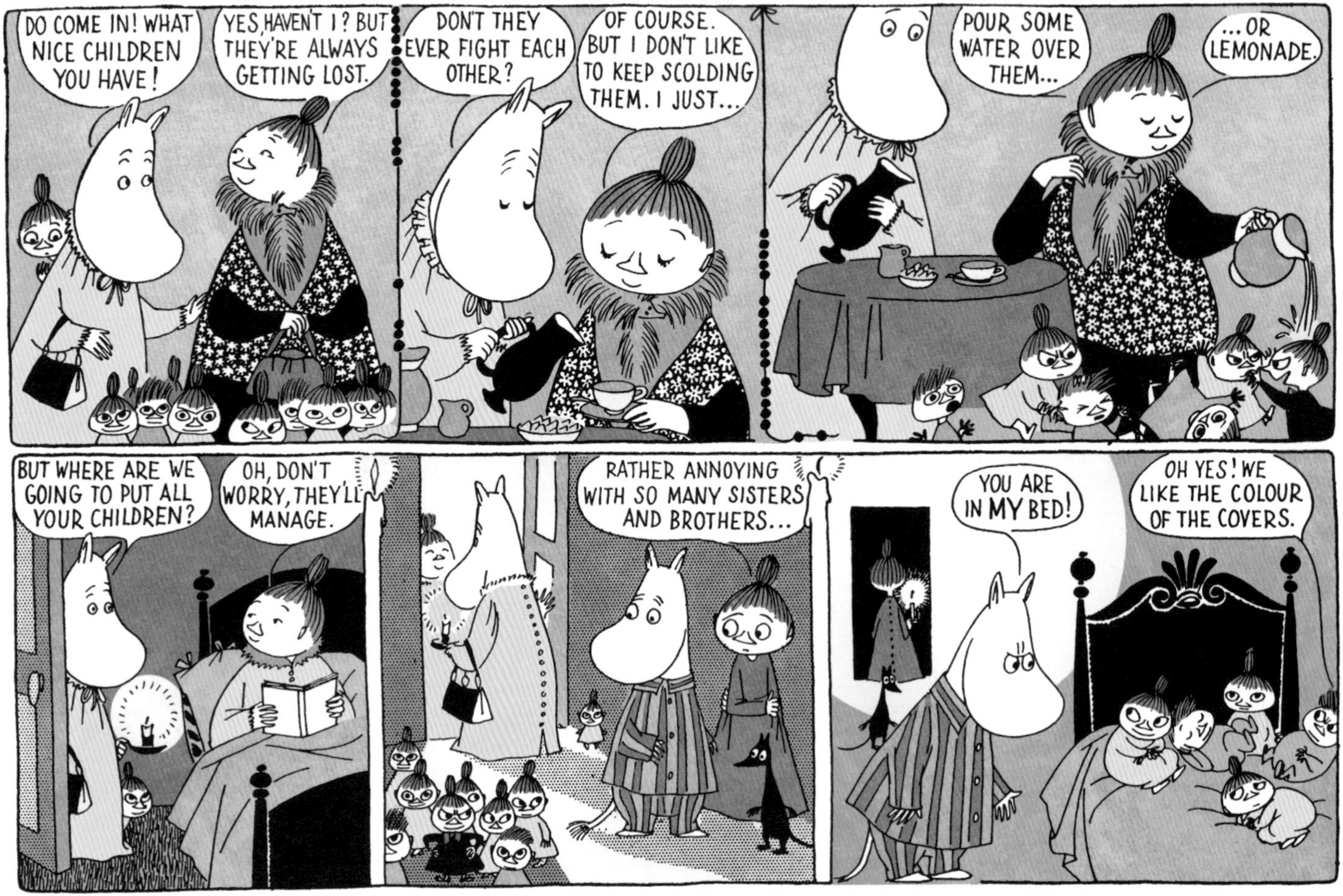
DO COME IN! WHAT NICE CHILDREN YOU HAVE!
YES, HAVEN'T I? BUT THEY'RE ALWAYS GETTING LOST.
DON'T THEY EVER FIGHT EACH OTHER?
OF COURSE. BUT I DON'T LIKE TO KEEP SCOLDING THEM. I JUST...
POUR SOME WATER OVER THEM...
...OR LEMONADE.
BUT WHERE ARE WE GOING TO PUT ALL YOUR CHILDREN?
OH, DON'T WORRY, THEY'LL MANAGE.
RATHER ANNOYING WITH SO MANY SISTERS AND BROTHERS...
YOU ARE IN MY BED!
OH YES! WE LIKE THE COLOUR OF THE COVERS.

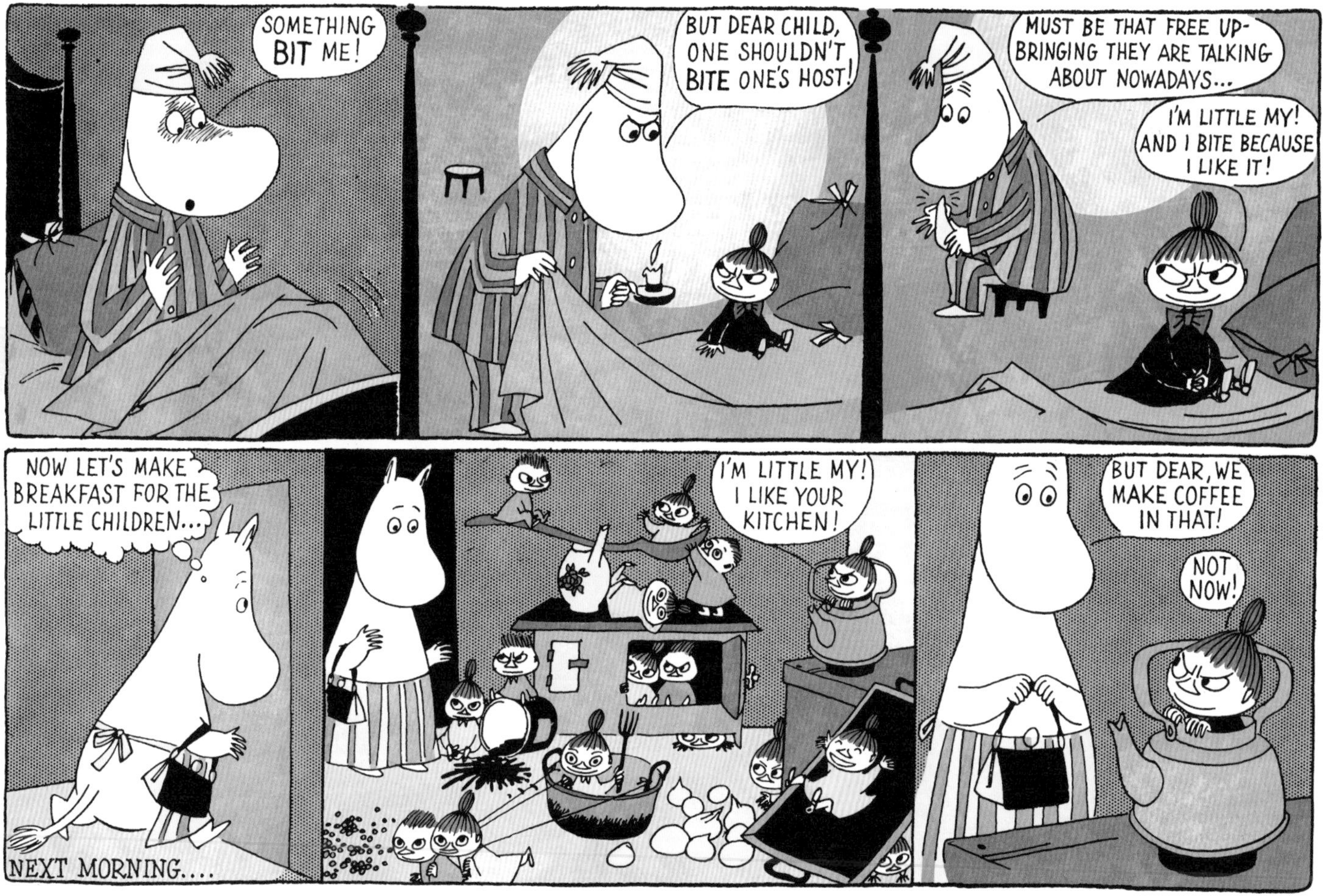
SOMETHING BIT ME!
BUT DEAR CHILD, ONE SHOULDN'T BITE ONE'S HOST!
MUST BE THAT FREE UP-BRINGING THEY ARE TALKING ABOUT NOWADAYS...
I'M LITTLE MY! AND I BITE BECAUSE I LIKE IT!
NOW LET'S MAKE BREAKFAST FOR THE LITTLE CHILDREN...
NEXT MORNING....
I'M LITTLE MY! I LIKE YOUR KITCHEN!
BUT DEAR, WE MAKE COFFEE IN THAT!
NOT NOW!

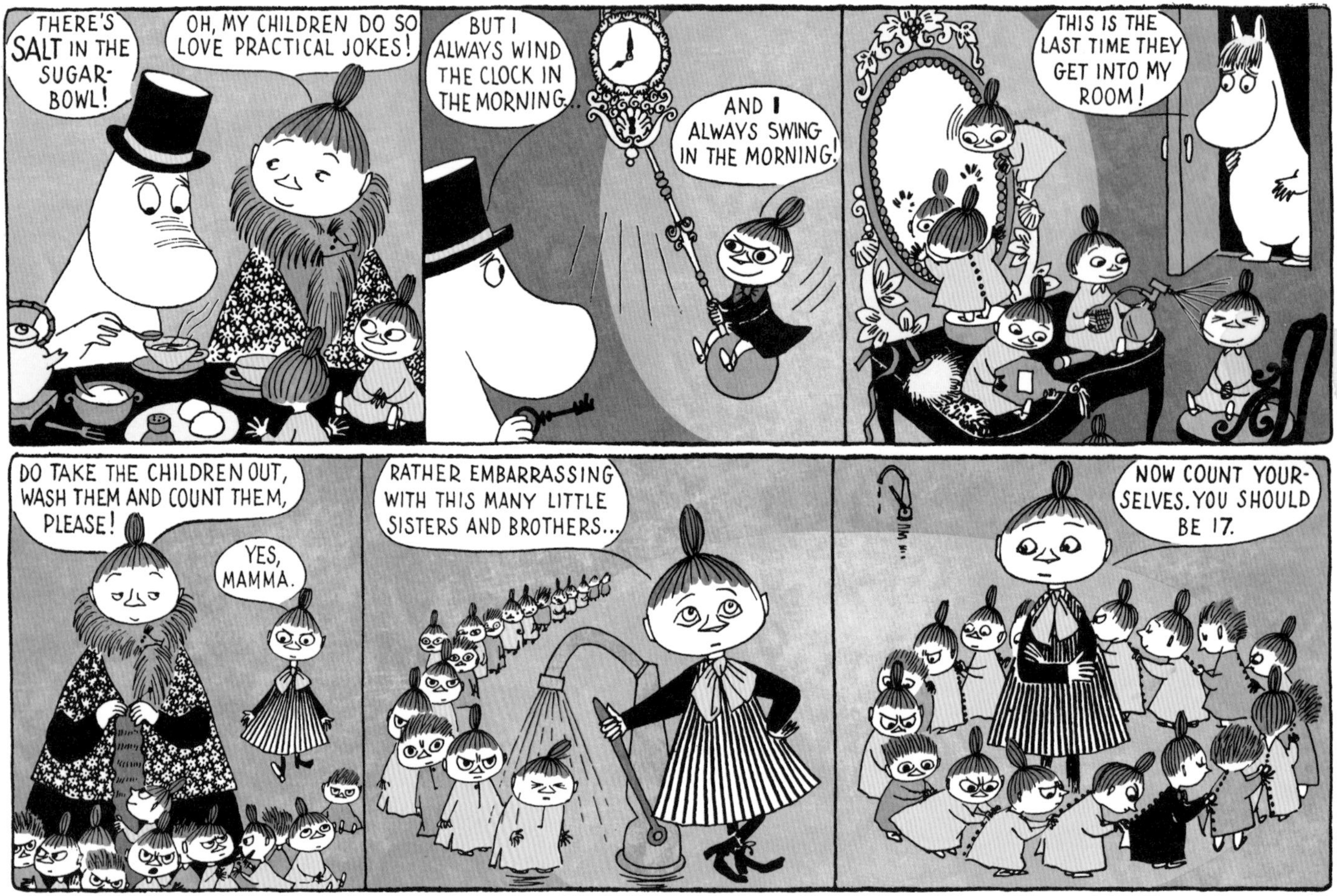
THERE'S SALT IN THE SUGAR-BOWL!
OH, MY CHILDREN DO SO LOVE PRACTICAL JOKES!
BUT I ALWAYS WIND THE CLOCK IN THE MORNING...
AND I ALWAYS SWING IN THE MORNING!
THIS IS THE LAST TIME THEY GET INTO MY ROOM!
DO TAKE THE CHILDREN OUT, WASH THEM AND COUNT THEM, PLEASE!
YES, MAMMA.
RATHER EMBARRASSING WITH THIS MANY LITTLE SISTERS AND BROTHERS...
NOW COUNT YOURSELVES. YOU SHOULD BE 17.

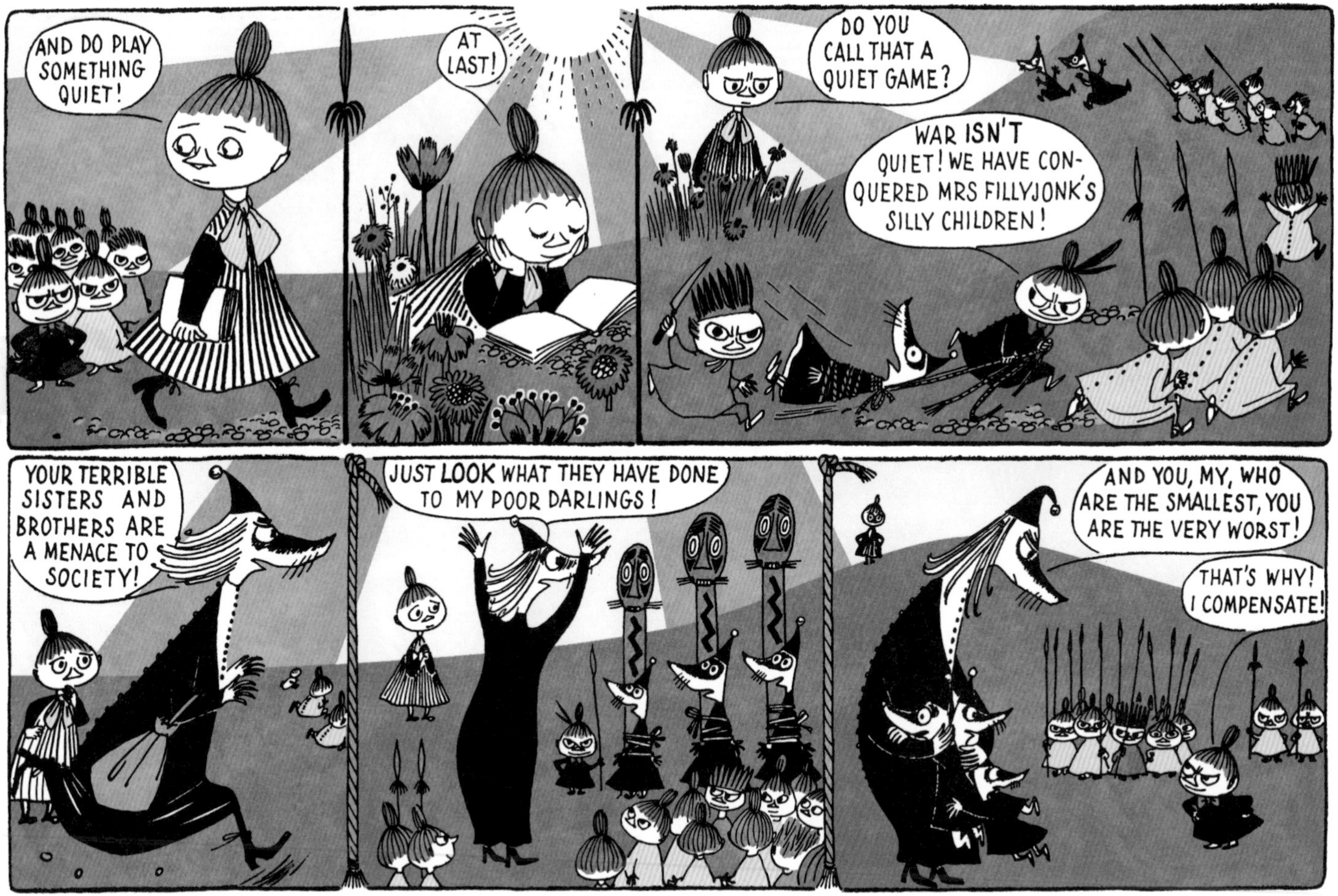
AND DO PLAY SOMETHING QUIET!
AT LAST!
DO YOU CALL THAT A QUIET GAME?
WAR ISN'T QUIET! WE HAVE CONQUERED MRS FILLYJONK'S SILLY CHILDREN!
YOUR TERRIBLE SISTERS AND BROTHERS ARE A MENACE TO SOCIETY!
JUST LOOK WHAT THEY HAVE DONE TO MY POOR DARLINGS!
AND YOU, MY, WHO ARE THE SMALLEST, YOU ARE THE VERY WORST!
THAT'S WHY! I COMPENSATE!

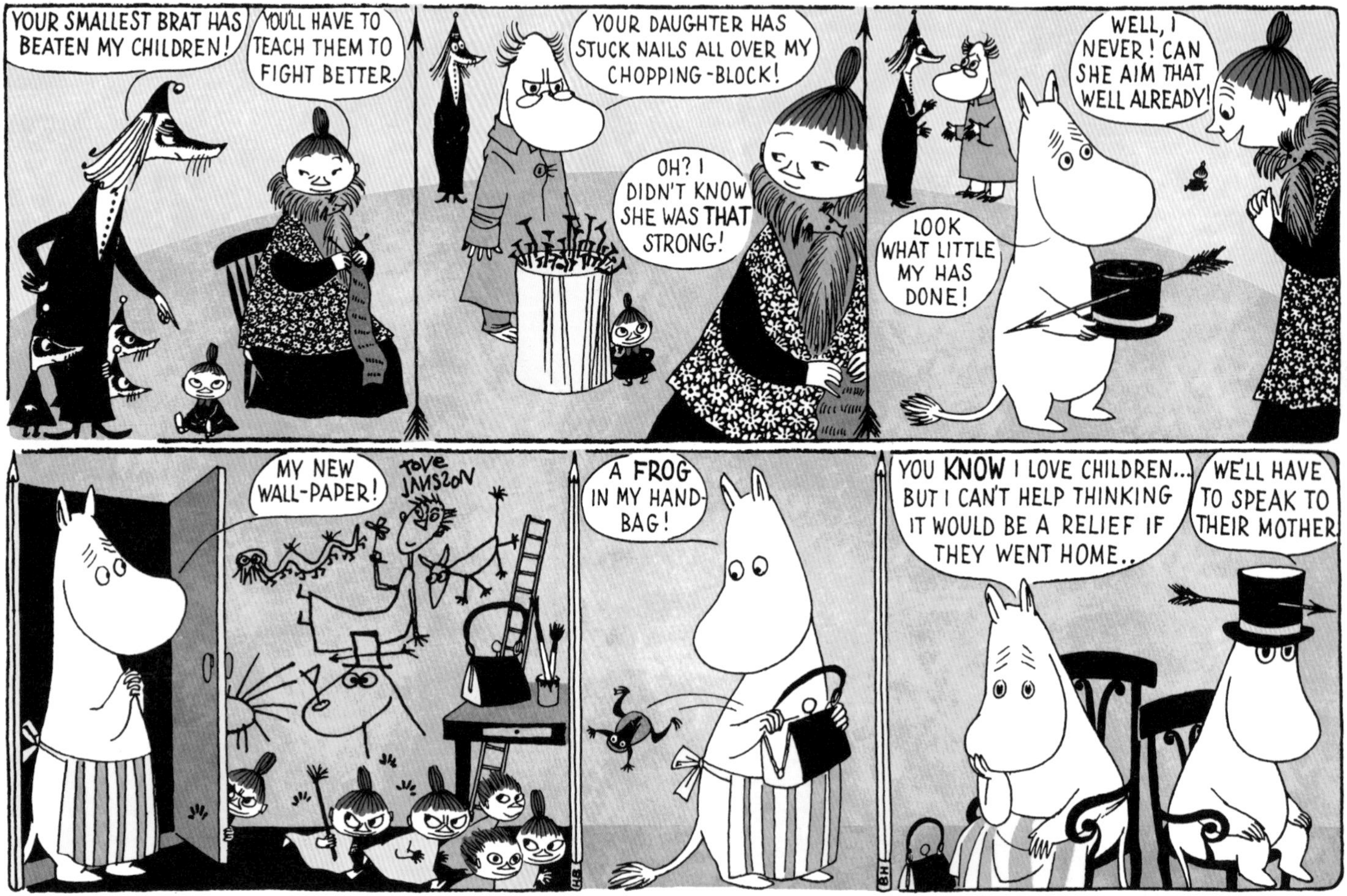
YOUR SMALLEST BRAT HAS BEATEN MY CHILDREN!
YOU'LL HAVE TO TEACH THEM TO FIGHT BETTER.
YOUR DAUGHTER HAS STUCK NAILS ALL OVER MY CHOPPING-BLOCK!
OH? I DIDN'T KNOW SHE WAS THAT STRONG!
LOOK WHAT LITTLE MY HAS DONE!
WELL, I NEVER! CAN SHE AIM THAT WELL ALREADY!
MY NEW WALL-PAPER!
TOVE JANSSON
A FROG IN MY HAND-BAG!
YOU KNOW I LOVE CHILDREN... BUT I CAN'T HELP THINKING IT WOULD BE A RELIEF IF THEY WENT HOME..
WE'LL HAVE TO SPEAK TO THEIR MOTHER

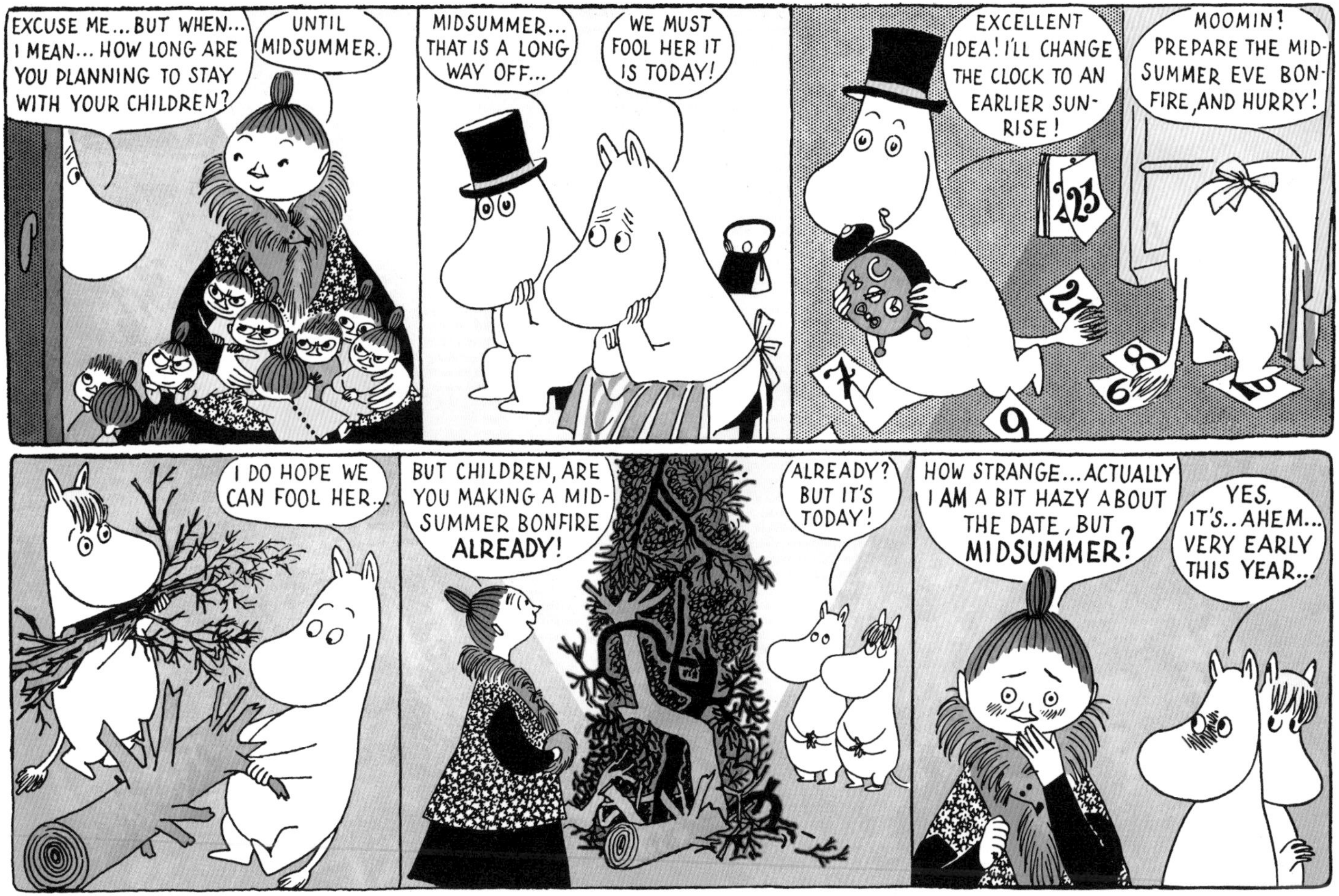
EXCUSE ME... BUT WHEN... I MEAN... HOW LONG ARE YOU PLANNING TO STAY WITH YOUR CHILDREN?
UNTIL MIDSUMMER.
MIDSUMMER... THAT IS A LONG WAY OFF...
WE MUST FOOL HER IT IS TODAY!
EXCELLENT IDEA! I'LL CHANGE THE CLOCK TO AN EARLIER SUN-RISE!
MOOMIN! PREPARE THE MID-SUMMER EVE BON-FIRE, AND HURRY!
I DO HOPE WE CAN FOOL HER...
BUT CHILDREN, ARE YOU MAKING A MID-SUMMER BONFIRE **ALREADY**!
ALREADY? BUT IT'S TODAY!
HOW STRANGE... ACTUALLY I **AM** A BIT HAZY ABOUT THE DATE, BUT **MIDSUMMER**?
YES, IT'S.. AHEM... VERY EARLY THIS YEAR...

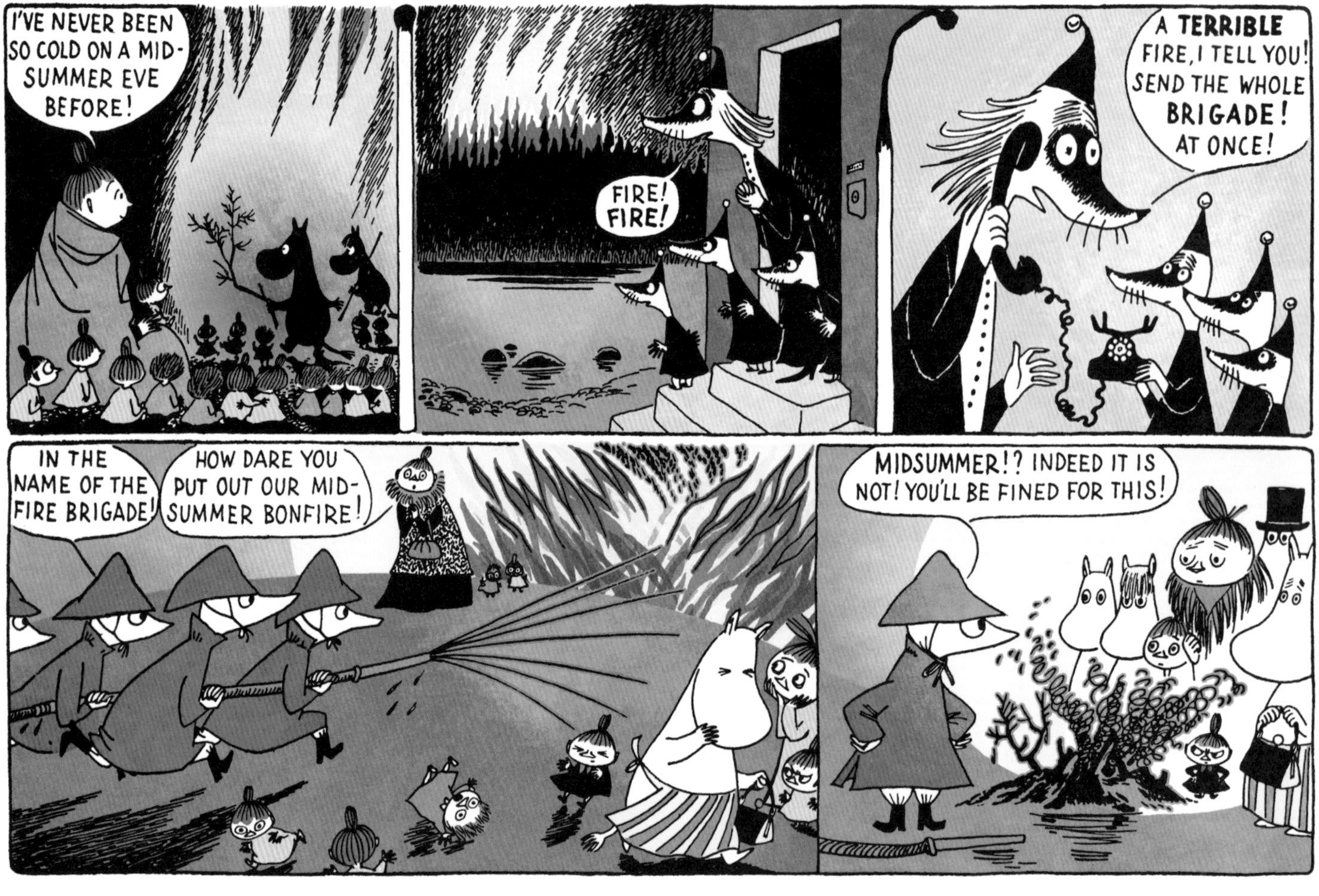
I'VE NEVER BEEN SO COLD ON A MID-SUMMER EVE BEFORE!
FIRE! FIRE!
A **TERRIBLE** FIRE, I TELL YOU! SEND THE WHOLE **BRIGADE!** AT ONCE!
IN THE NAME OF THE FIRE BRIGADE!
HOW DARE YOU PUT OUT OUR MID-SUMMER BONFIRE!
MIDSUMMER!? INDEED IT IS NOT! YOU'LL BE FINED FOR THIS!

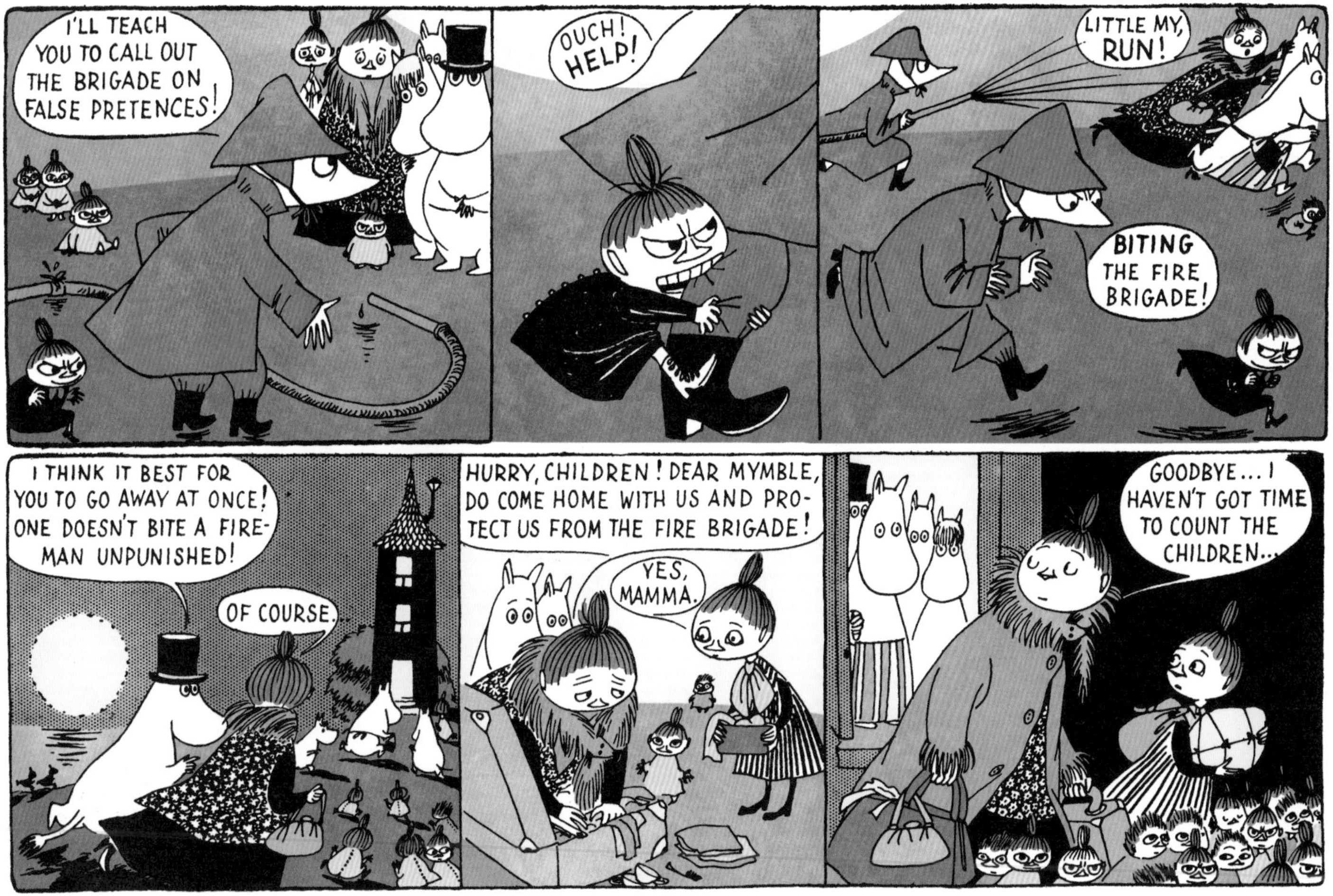
I'LL TEACH YOU TO CALL OUT THE BRIGADE ON FALSE PRETENCES!
OUCH! HELP!
LITTLE MY, RUN!
BITING THE FIRE BRIGADE!
I THINK IT BEST FOR YOU TO GO AWAY AT ONCE! ONE DOESN'T BITE A FIRE-MAN UNPUNISHED!
OF COURSE...
HURRY, CHILDREN! DEAR MYMBLE, DO COME HOME WITH US AND PRO-TECT US FROM THE FIRE BRIGADE!
YES, MAMMA.
GOODBYE... I HAVEN'T GOT TIME TO COUNT THE CHILDREN...

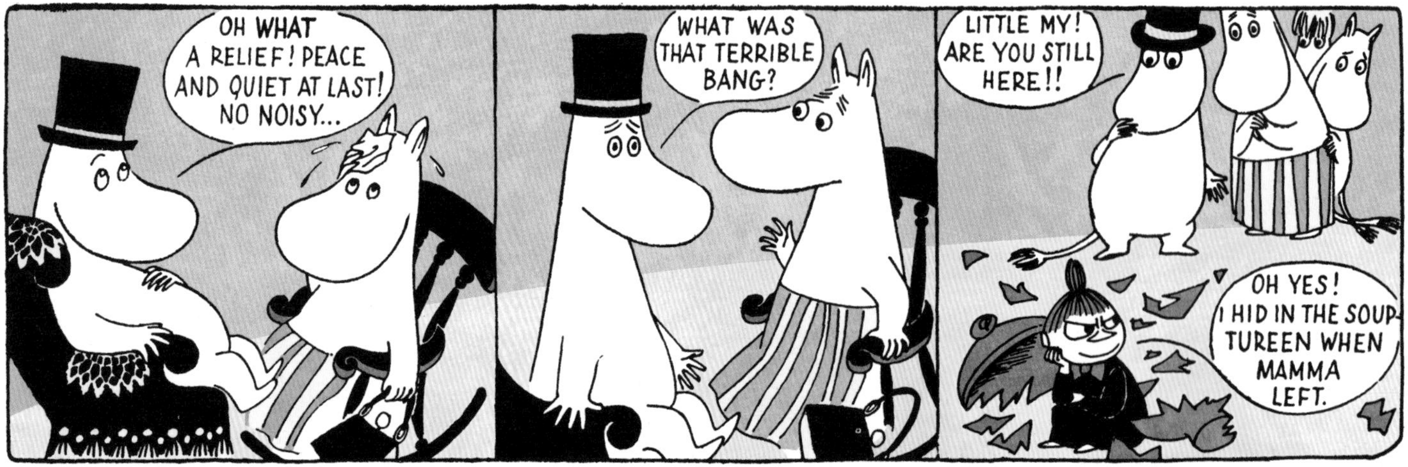
OH WHAT A RELIEF! PEACE AND QUIET AT LAST! NO NOISY...
WHAT WAS THAT TERRIBLE BANG?
LITTLE MY! ARE YOU STILL HERE!!
OH YES! I HID IN THE SOUP-TUREEN WHEN MAMMA LEFT.

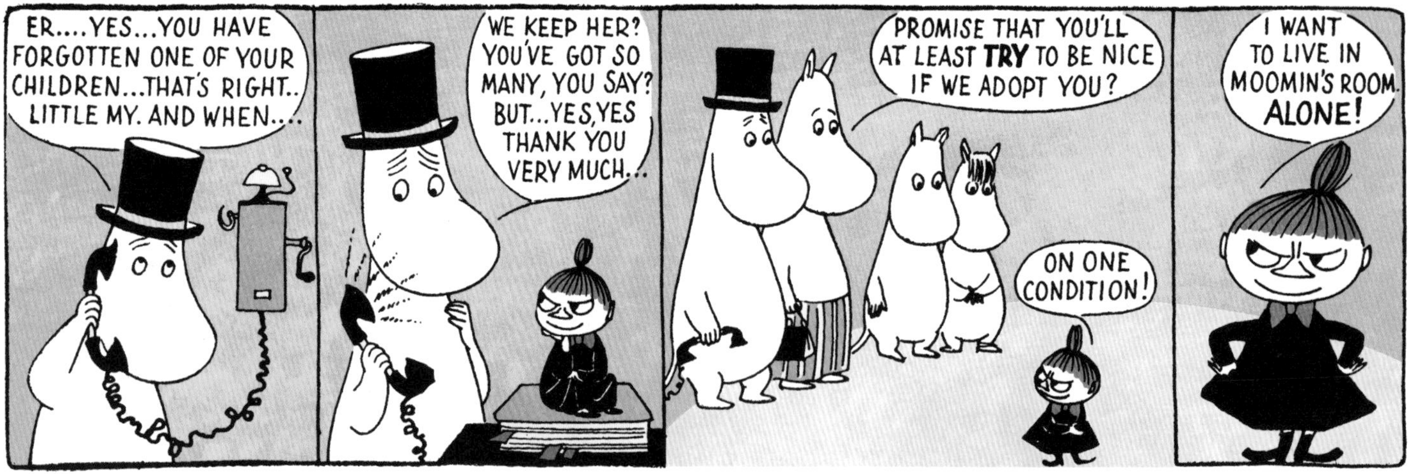
ER....YES...YOU HAVE FORGOTTEN ONE OF YOUR CHILDREN...THAT'S RIGHT.. LITTLE MY. AND WHEN....
WE KEEP HER? YOU'VE GOT SO MANY, YOU SAY? BUT...YES,YES THANK YOU VERY MUCH...
PROMISE THAT YOU'LL AT LEAST TRY TO BE NICE IF WE ADOPT YOU?
ON ONE CONDITION!
I WANT TO LIVE IN MOOMIN'S ROOM. ALONE!

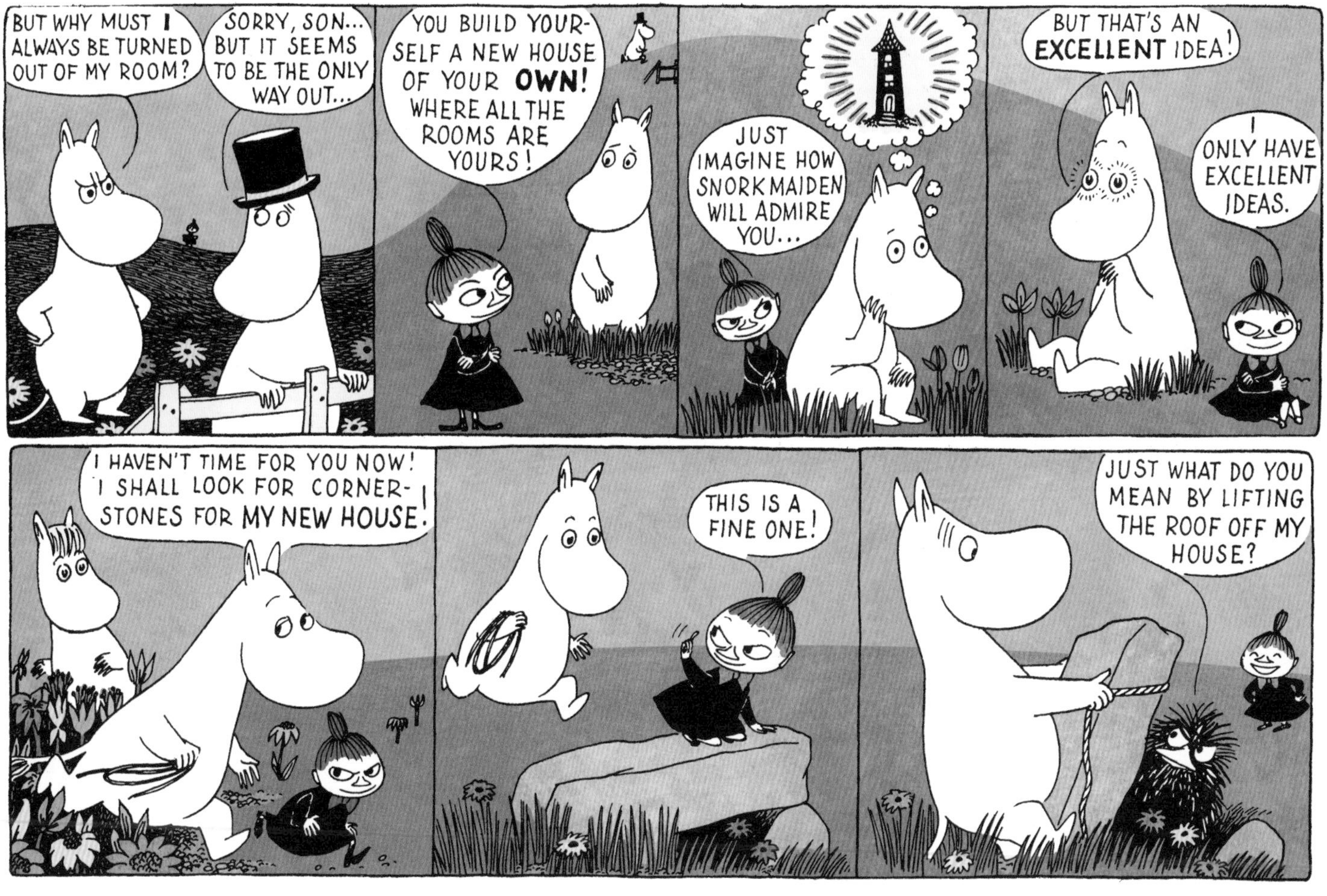
BUT WHY MUST I ALWAYS BE TURNED OUT OF MY ROOM?
SORRY, SON... BUT IT SEEMS TO BE THE ONLY WAY OUT...
YOU BUILD YOURSELF A NEW HOUSE OF YOUR OWN! WHERE ALL THE ROOMS ARE YOURS!
JUST IMAGINE HOW SNORKMAIDEN WILL ADMIRE YOU...
BUT THAT'S AN EXCELLENT IDEA!
I ONLY HAVE EXCELLENT IDEAS.
I HAVEN'T TIME FOR YOU NOW! I SHALL LOOK FOR CORNER-STONES FOR MY NEW HOUSE!
THIS IS A FINE ONE!
JUST WHAT DO YOU MEAN BY LIFTING THE ROOF OFF MY HOUSE?

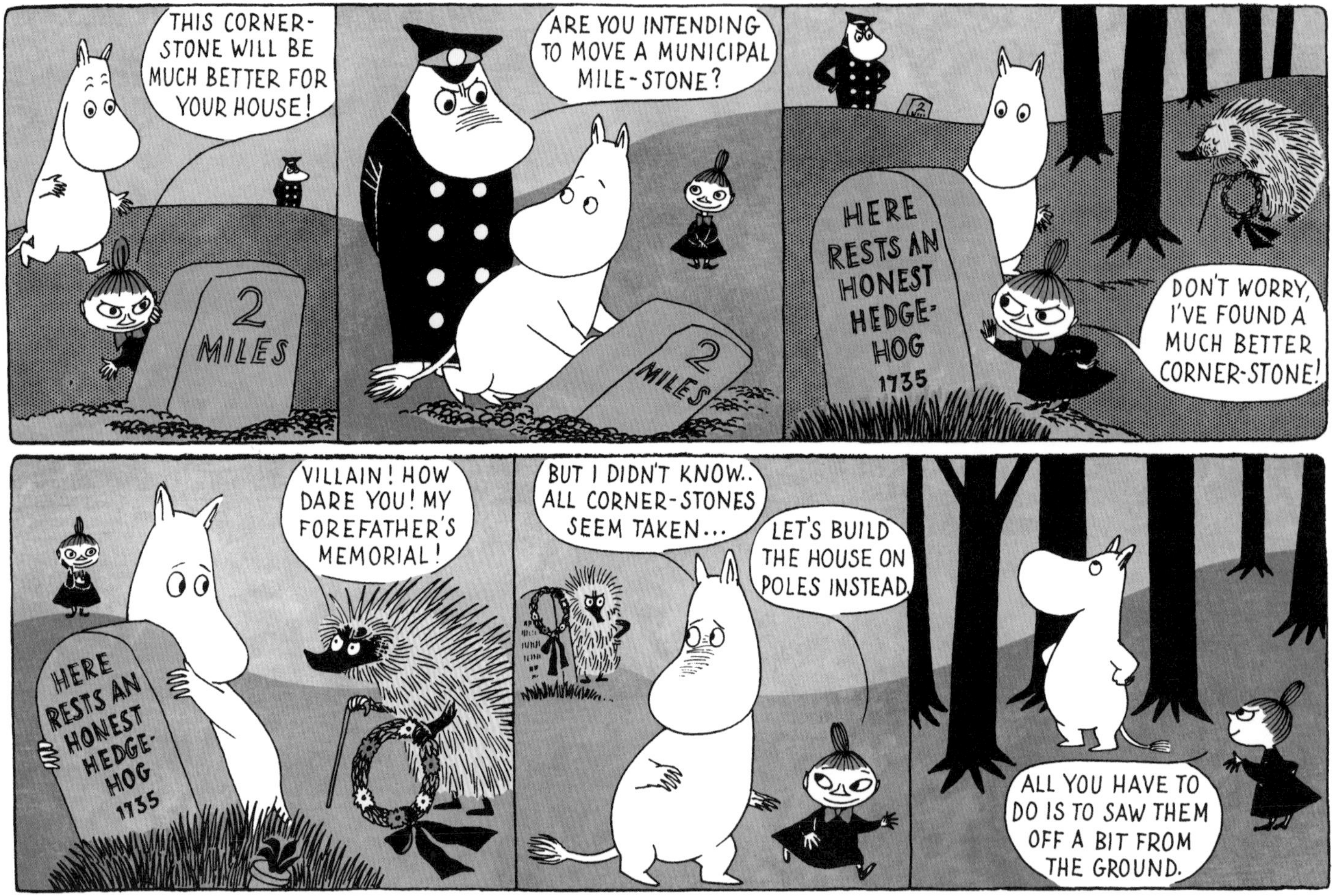
THIS CORNER-STONE WILL BE MUCH BETTER FOR YOUR HOUSE!
2 MILES
ARE YOU INTENDING TO MOVE A MUNICIPAL MILE-STONE?
2 MILES
HERE RESTS AN HONEST HEDGE-HOG 1735
DON'T WORRY, I'VE FOUND A MUCH BETTER CORNER-STONE!
VILLAIN! HOW DARE YOU! MY FOREFATHER'S MEMORIAL!
HERE RESTS AN HONEST HEDGE-HOG 1735
BUT I DIDN'T KNOW.. ALL CORNER-STONES SEEM TAKEN...
LET'S BUILD THE HOUSE ON POLES INSTEAD.
ALL YOU HAVE TO DO IS TO SAW THEM OFF A BIT FROM THE GROUND.

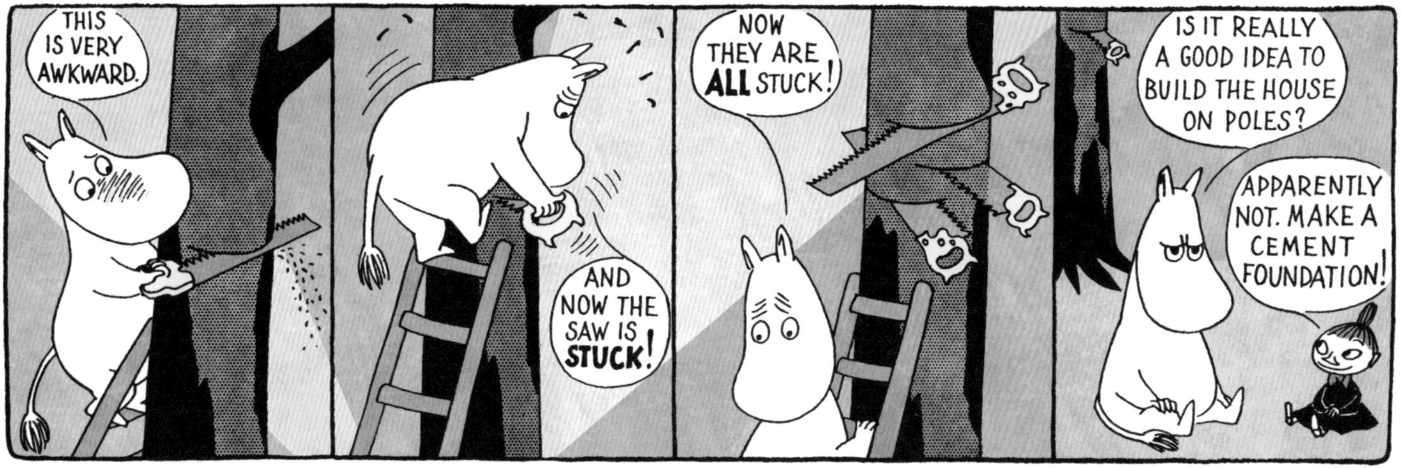
THIS IS VERY AWKWARD.
AND NOW THE SAW IS STUCK!
NOW THEY ARE ALL STUCK!
IS IT REALLY A GOOD IDEA TO BUILD THE HOUSE ON POLES?
APPARENTLY NOT. MAKE A CEMENT FOUNDATION!

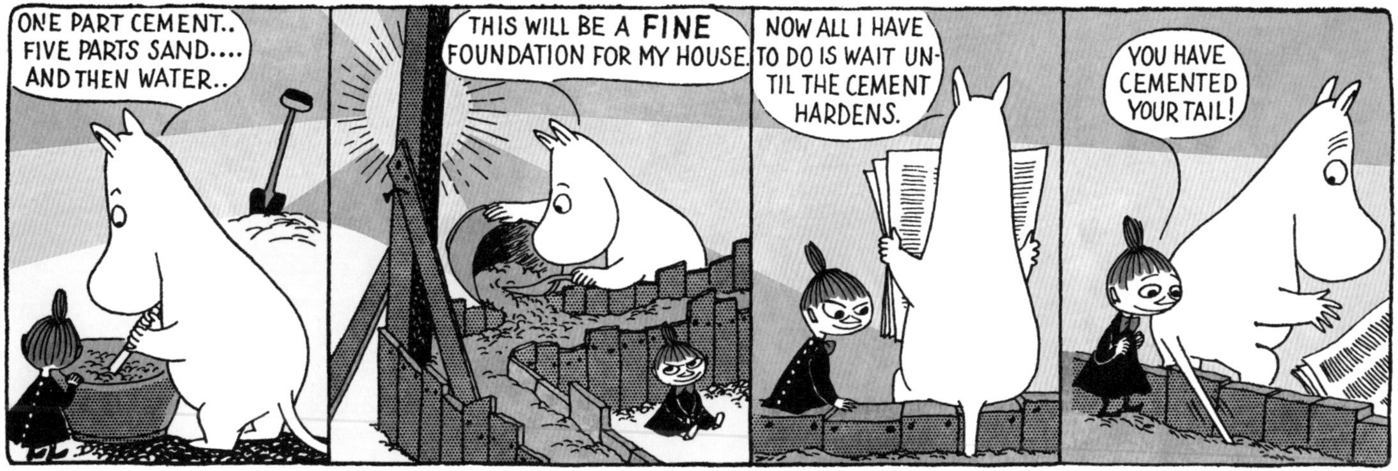
ONE PART CEMENT.. FIVE PARTS SAND.... AND THEN WATER..
THIS WILL BE A FINE FOUNDATION FOR MY HOUSE.
NOW ALL I HAVE TO DO IS WAIT UNTIL THE CEMENT HARDENS.
YOU HAVE CEMENTED YOUR TAIL!

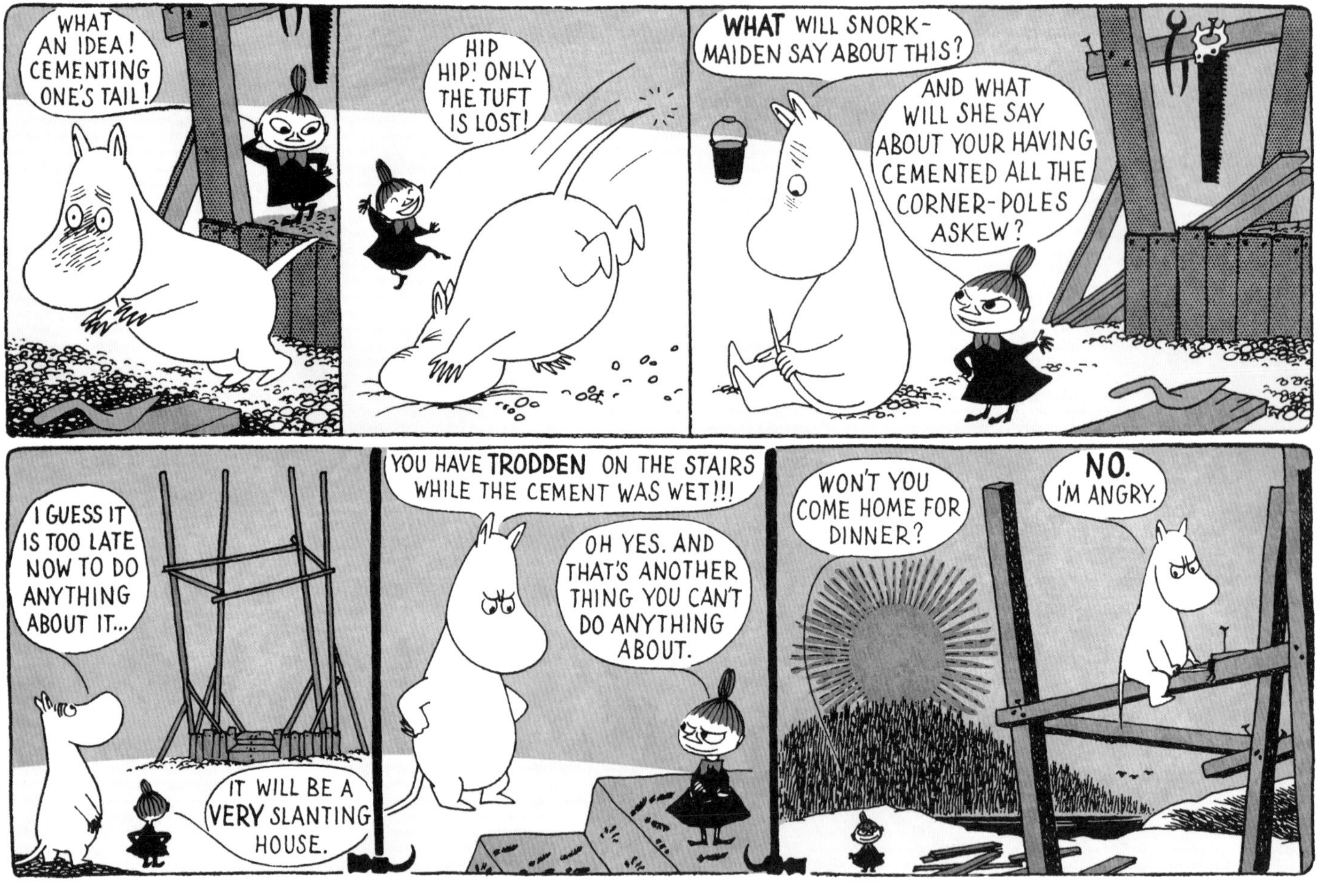
WHAT AN IDEA! CEMENTING ONE'S TAIL!
HIP HIP! ONLY THE TUFT IS LOST!
WHAT WILL SNORK-MAIDEN SAY ABOUT THIS?
AND WHAT WILL SHE SAY ABOUT YOUR HAVING CEMENTED ALL THE CORNER-POLES ASKEW?
I GUESS IT IS TOO LATE NOW TO DO ANYTHING ABOUT IT...
IT WILL BE A VERY SLANTING HOUSE.
YOU HAVE TRODDEN ON THE STAIRS WHILE THE CEMENT WAS WET!!!
OH YES. AND THAT'S ANOTHER THING YOU CAN'T DO ANYTHING ABOUT.
WON'T YOU COME HOME FOR DINNER?
NO. I'M ANGRY.

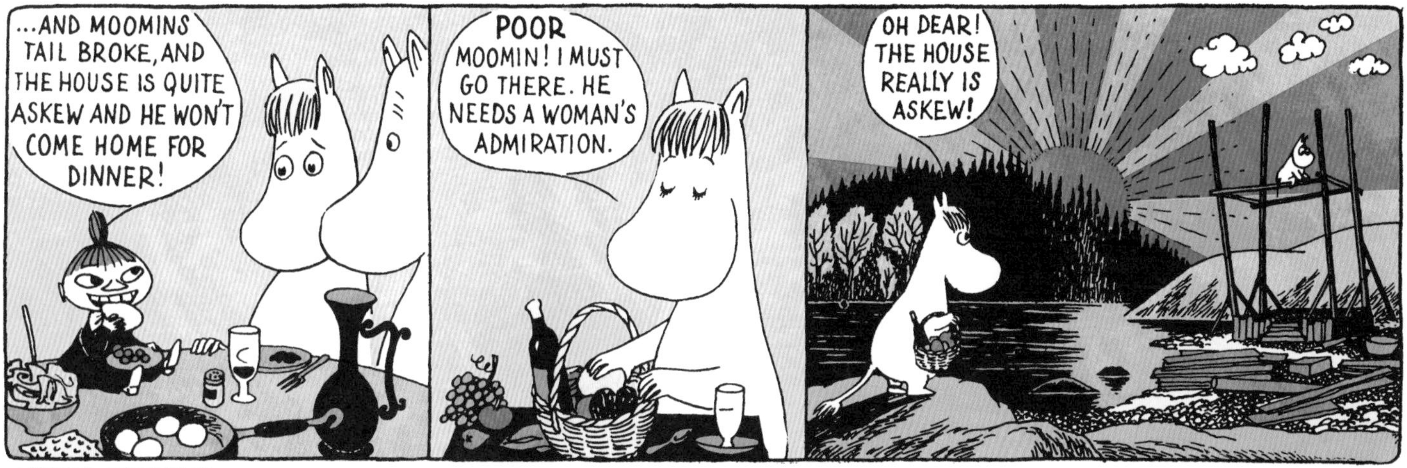
...AND MOOMINS TAIL BROKE, AND THE HOUSE IS QUITE ASKEW AND HE WON'T COME HOME FOR DINNER!
POOR MOOMIN! I MUST GO THERE. HE NEEDS A WOMAN'S ADMIRATION.
OH DEAR! THE HOUSE REALLY IS ASKEW!

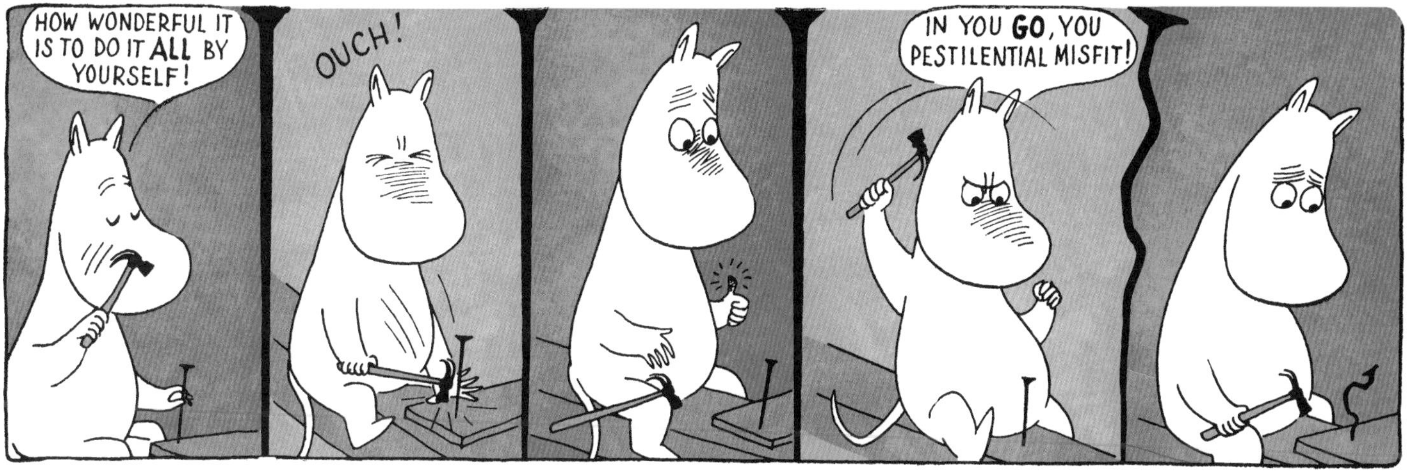
HOW WONDERFUL IT IS TO DO IT ALL BY YOURSELF!
OUCH!
IN YOU GO, YOU PESTILENTIAL MISFIT!

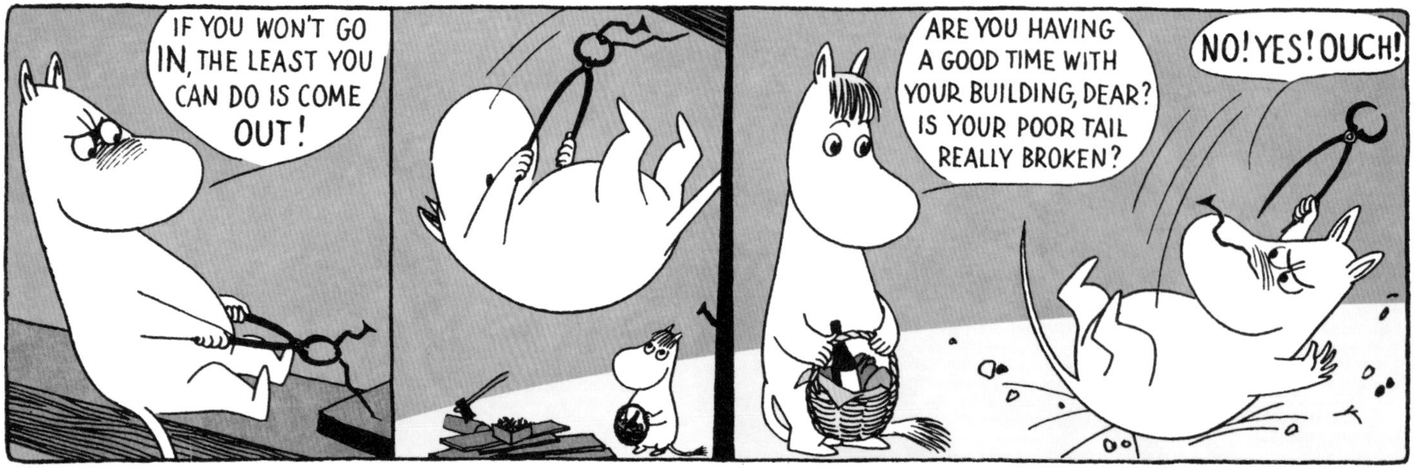

IF YOU WON'T GO IN, THE LEAST YOU CAN DO IS COME OUT!
ARE YOU HAVING A GOOD TIME WITH YOUR BUILDING, DEAR? IS YOUR POOR TAIL REALLY BROKEN?
NO! YES! OUCH!

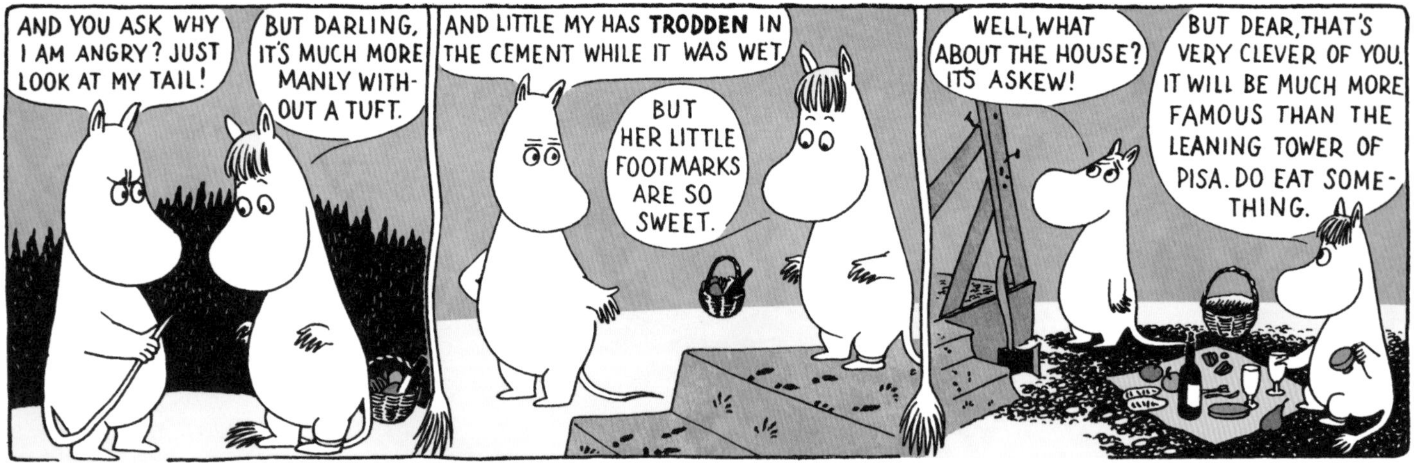

AND YOU ASK WHY I AM ANGRY? JUST LOOK AT MY TAIL!
BUT DARLING, IT'S MUCH MORE MANLY WITHOUT A TUFT.
AND LITTLE MY HAS TRODDEN IN THE CEMENT WHILE IT WAS WET.
BUT HER LITTLE FOOTMARKS ARE SO SWEET.
WELL, WHAT ABOUT THE HOUSE? IT'S ASKEW!
BUT DEAR, THAT'S VERY CLEVER OF YOU. IT WILL BE MUCH MORE FAMOUS THAN THE LEANING TOWER OF PISA. DO EAT SOMETHING.

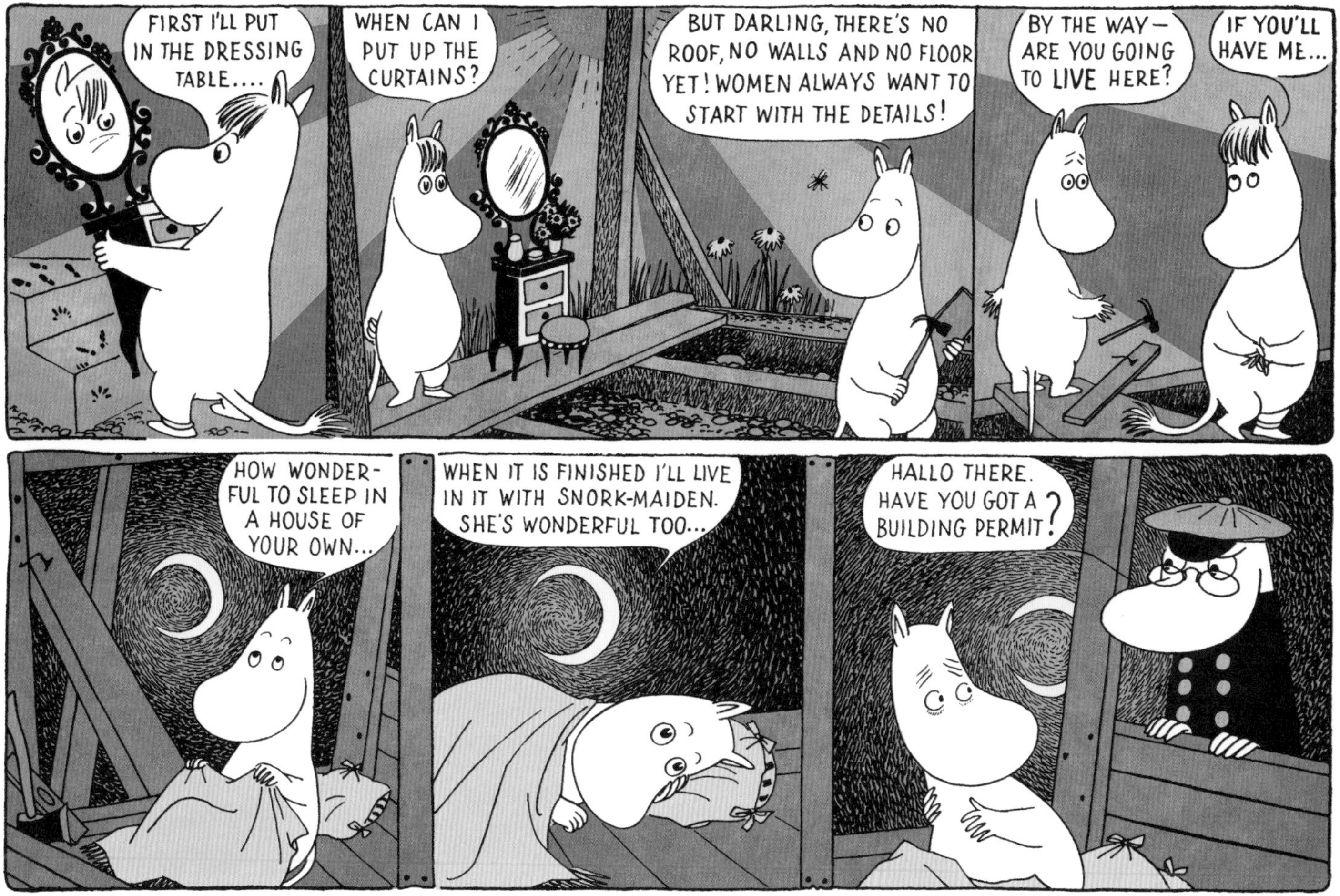
FIRST I'LL PUT IN THE DRESSING TABLE....
WHEN CAN I PUT UP THE CURTAINS?
BUT DARLING, THERE'S NO ROOF, NO WALLS AND NO FLOOR YET! WOMEN ALWAYS WANT TO START WITH THE DETAILS!
BY THE WAY— ARE YOU GOING TO LIVE HERE?
IF YOU'LL HAVE ME...
HOW WONDER-FUL TO SLEEP IN A HOUSE OF YOUR OWN...
WHEN IT IS FINISHED I'LL LIVE IN IT WITH SNORK-MAIDEN. SHE'S WONDERFUL TOO...
HALLO THERE. HAVE YOU GOT A BUILDING PERMIT?

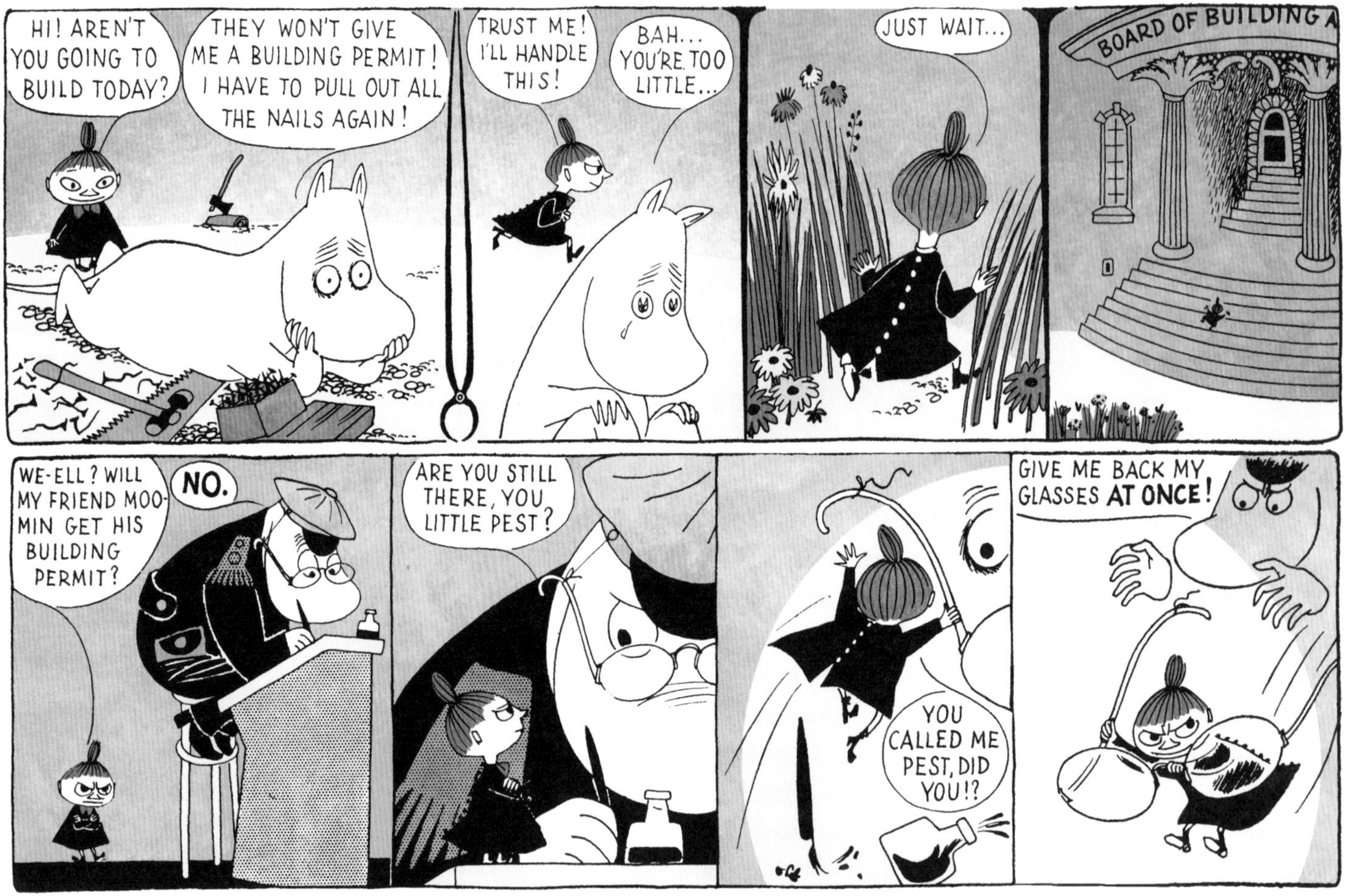
HI! AREN'T YOU GOING TO BUILD TODAY?
THEY WON'T GIVE ME A BUILDING PERMIT! I HAVE TO PULL OUT ALL THE NAILS AGAIN!
TRUST ME! I'LL HANDLE THIS!
BAH... YOU'RE TOO LITTLE...
JUST WAIT...
BOARD OF BUILDING A
WE-ELL? WILL MY FRIEND MOO-MIN GET HIS BUILDING PERMIT?
NO.
ARE YOU STILL THERE, YOU LITTLE PEST?
YOU CALLED ME PEST, DID YOU!?
GIVE ME BACK MY GLASSES AT ONCE!

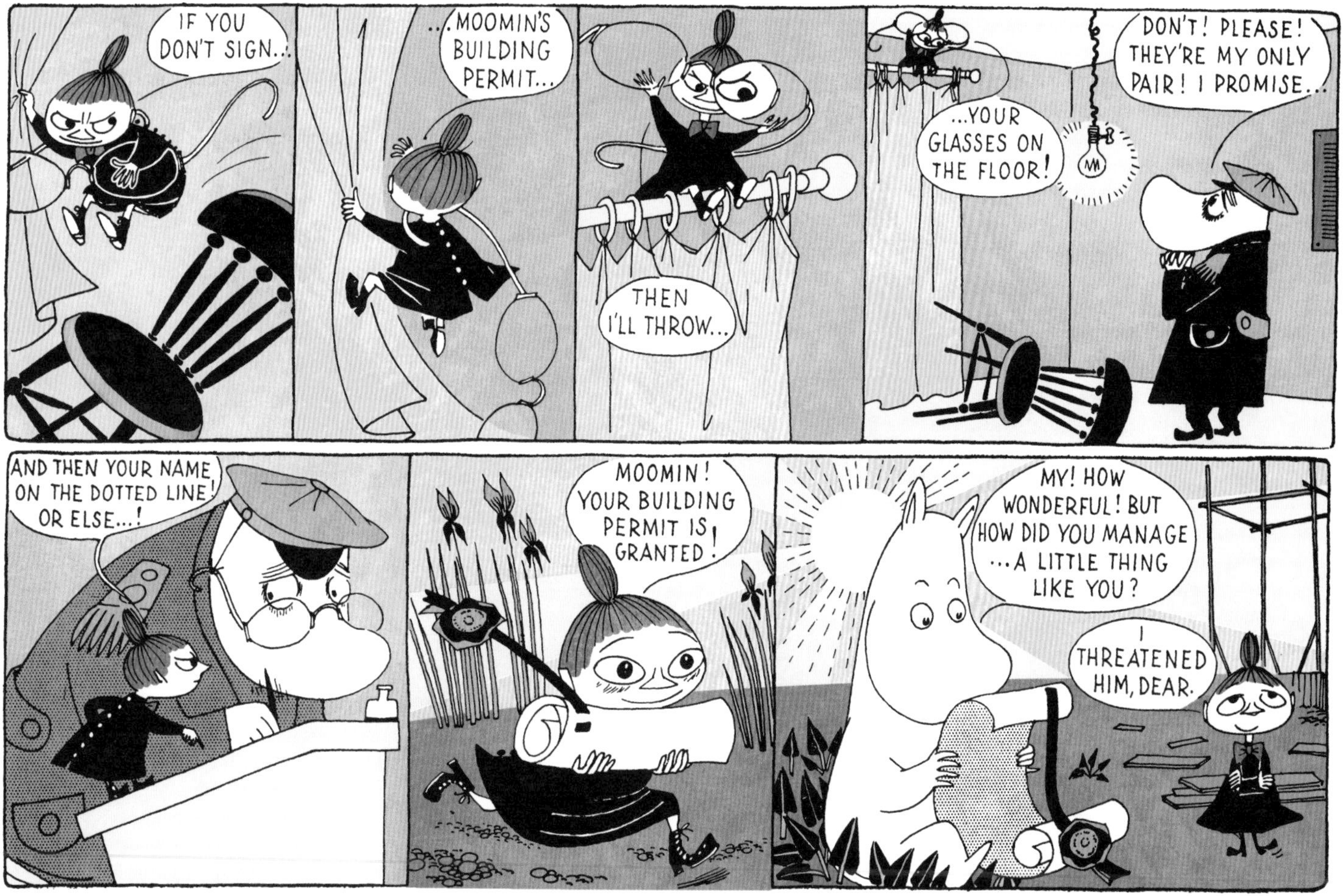
IF YOU DON'T SIGN...
...MOOMIN'S BUILDING PERMIT...
THEN I'LL THROW...
...YOUR GLASSES ON THE FLOOR!
DON'T! PLEASE! THEY'RE MY ONLY PAIR! I PROMISE...
AND THEN YOUR NAME ON THE DOTTED LINE! OR ELSE...!
MOOMIN! YOUR BUILDING PERMIT IS GRANTED!
MY! HOW WONDERFUL! BUT HOW DID YOU MANAGE ...A LITTLE THING LIKE YOU?
I THREATENED HIM, DEAR.

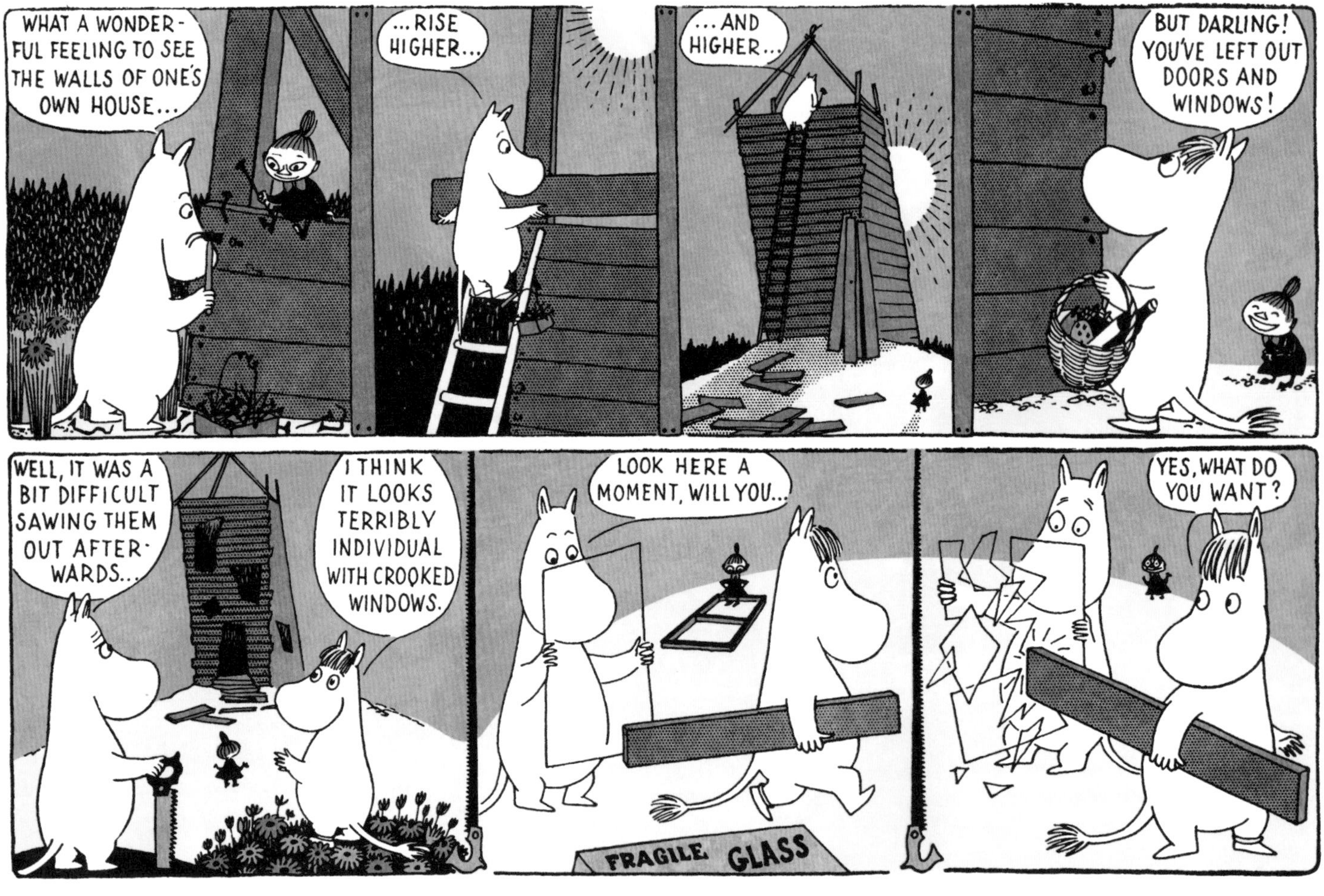
WHAT A WONDER-FUL FEELING TO SEE THE WALLS OF ONE'S OWN HOUSE...
...RISE HIGHER...
...AND HIGHER...
BUT DARLING! YOU'VE LEFT OUT DOORS AND WINDOWS!
WELL, IT WAS A BIT DIFFICULT SAWING THEM OUT AFTER-WARDS...
I THINK IT LOOKS TERRIBLY INDIVIDUAL WITH CROOKED WINDOWS.
LOOK HERE A MOMENT, WILL YOU...
FRAGILE GLASS
YES, WHAT DO YOU WANT?

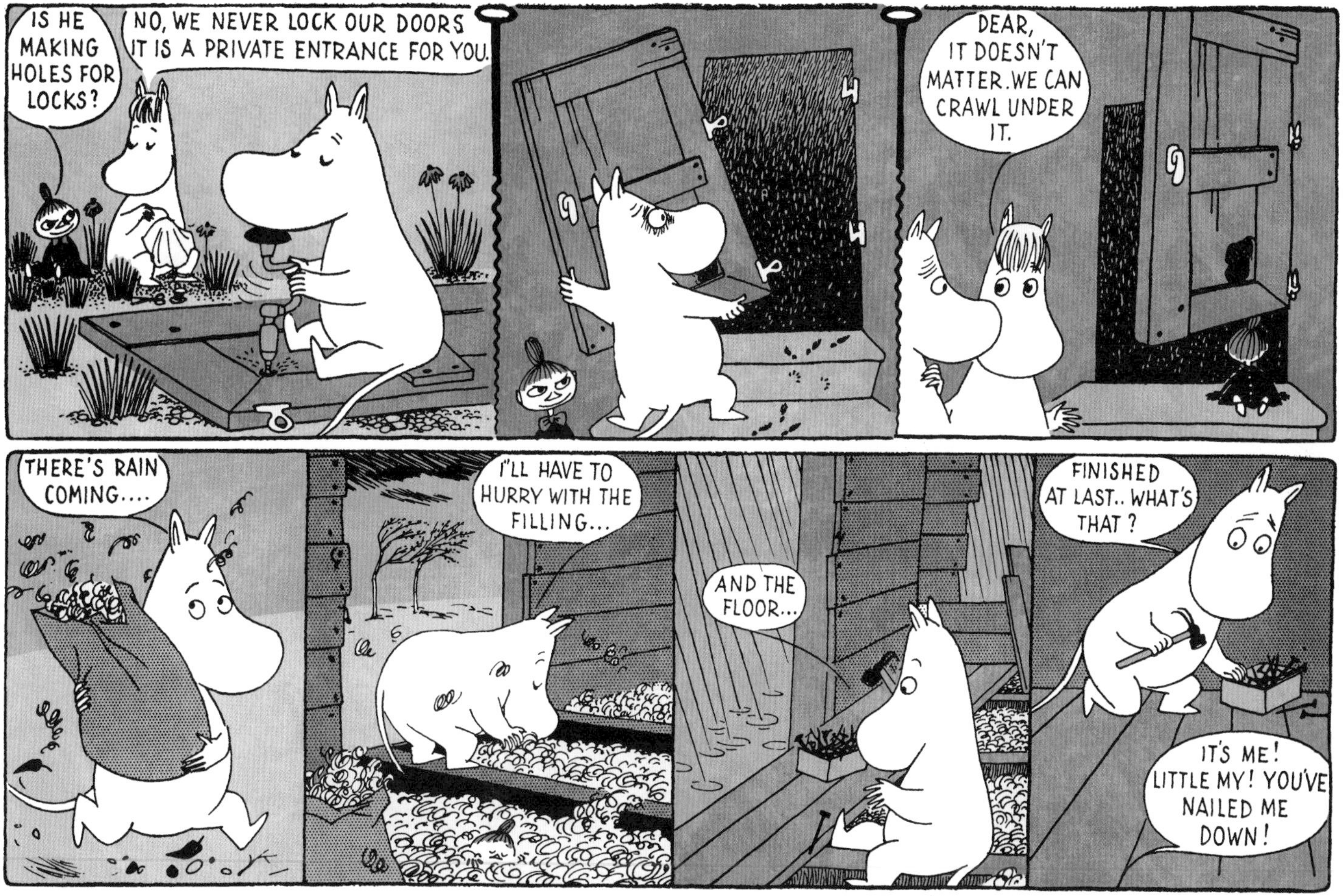
IS HE MAKING HOLES FOR LOCKS?
NO, WE NEVER LOCK OUR DOORS IT IS A PRIVATE ENTRANCE FOR YOU.
DEAR, IT DOESN'T MATTER. WE CAN CRAWL UNDER IT.
THERE'S RAIN COMING....
I'LL HAVE TO HURRY WITH THE FILLING...
AND THE FLOOR...
FINISHED AT LAST.. WHAT'S THAT?
IT'S ME! LITTLE MY! YOU'VE NAILED ME DOWN!

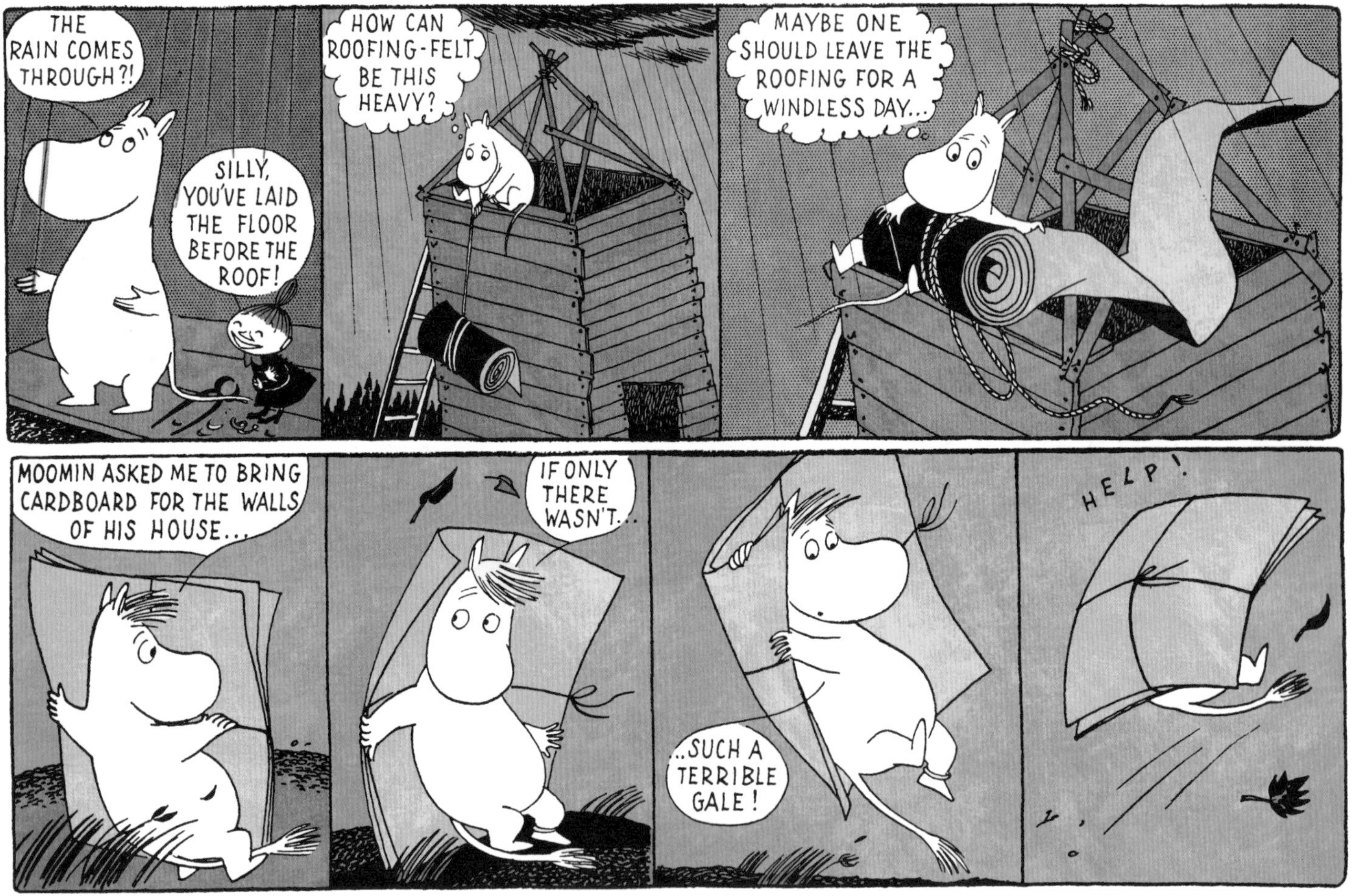
THE RAIN COMES THROUGH?!
SILLY, YOU'VE LAID THE FLOOR BEFORE THE ROOF!
HOW CAN ROOFING-FELT BE THIS HEAVY?
MAYBE ONE SHOULD LEAVE THE ROOFING FOR A WINDLESS DAY...
MOOMIN ASKED ME TO BRING CARDBOARD FOR THE WALLS OF HIS HOUSE...
IF ONLY THERE WASN'T...
..SUCH A TERRIBLE GALE!
HELP!

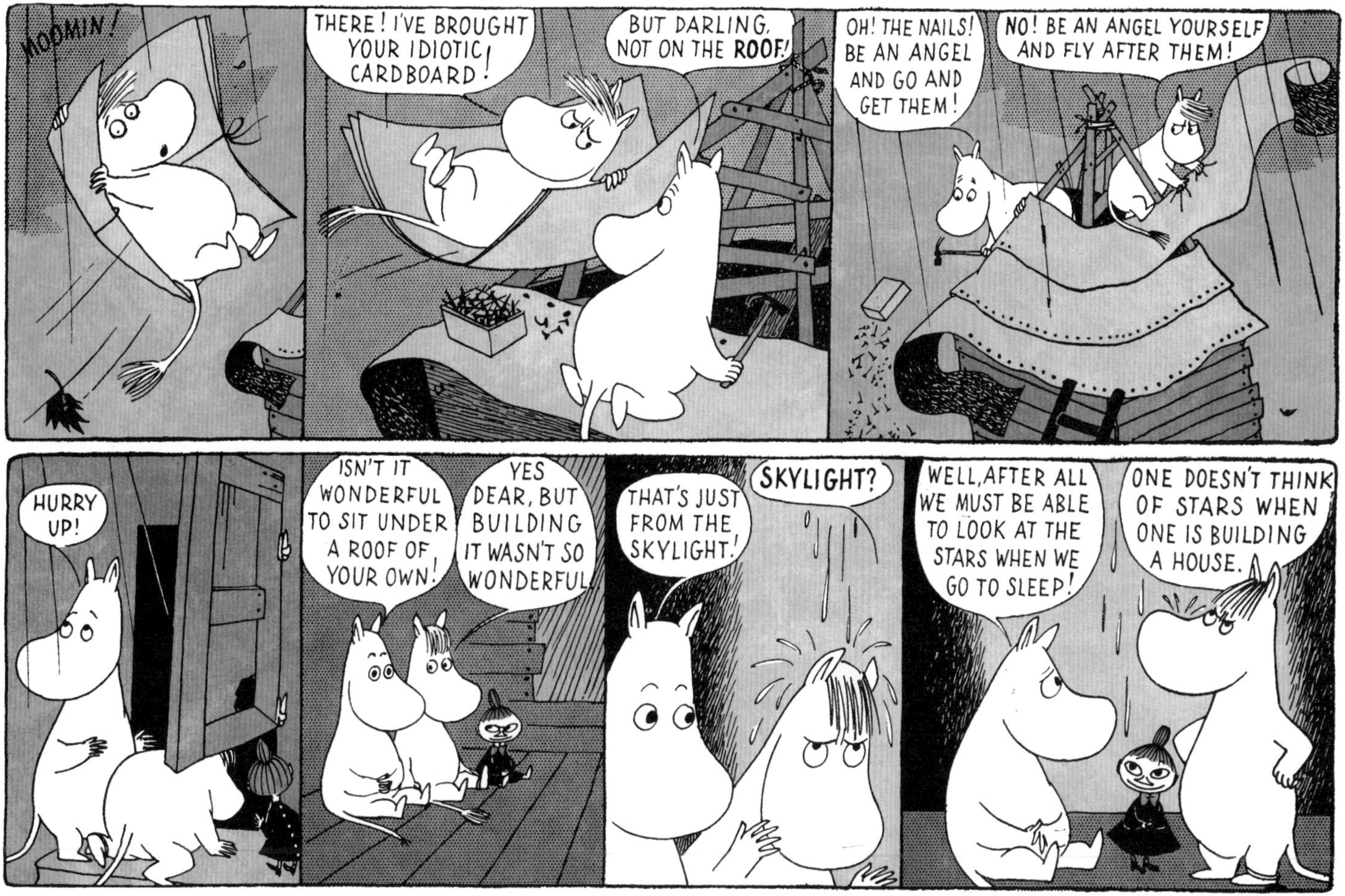
MOOMIN!
THERE! I'VE BROUGHT YOUR IDIOTIC CARDBOARD!
BUT DARLING, NOT ON THE ROOF!
OH! THE NAILS! BE AN ANGEL AND GO AND GET THEM!
NO! BE AN ANGEL YOURSELF AND FLY AFTER THEM!
HURRY UP!
ISN'T IT WONDERFUL TO SIT UNDER A ROOF OF YOUR OWN!
YES DEAR, BUT BUILDING IT WASN'T SO WONDERFUL.
THAT'S JUST FROM THE SKYLIGHT!
SKYLIGHT?
WELL, AFTER ALL WE MUST BE ABLE TO LOOK AT THE STARS WHEN WE GO TO SLEEP!
ONE DOESN'T THINK OF STARS WHEN ONE IS BUILDING A HOUSE.

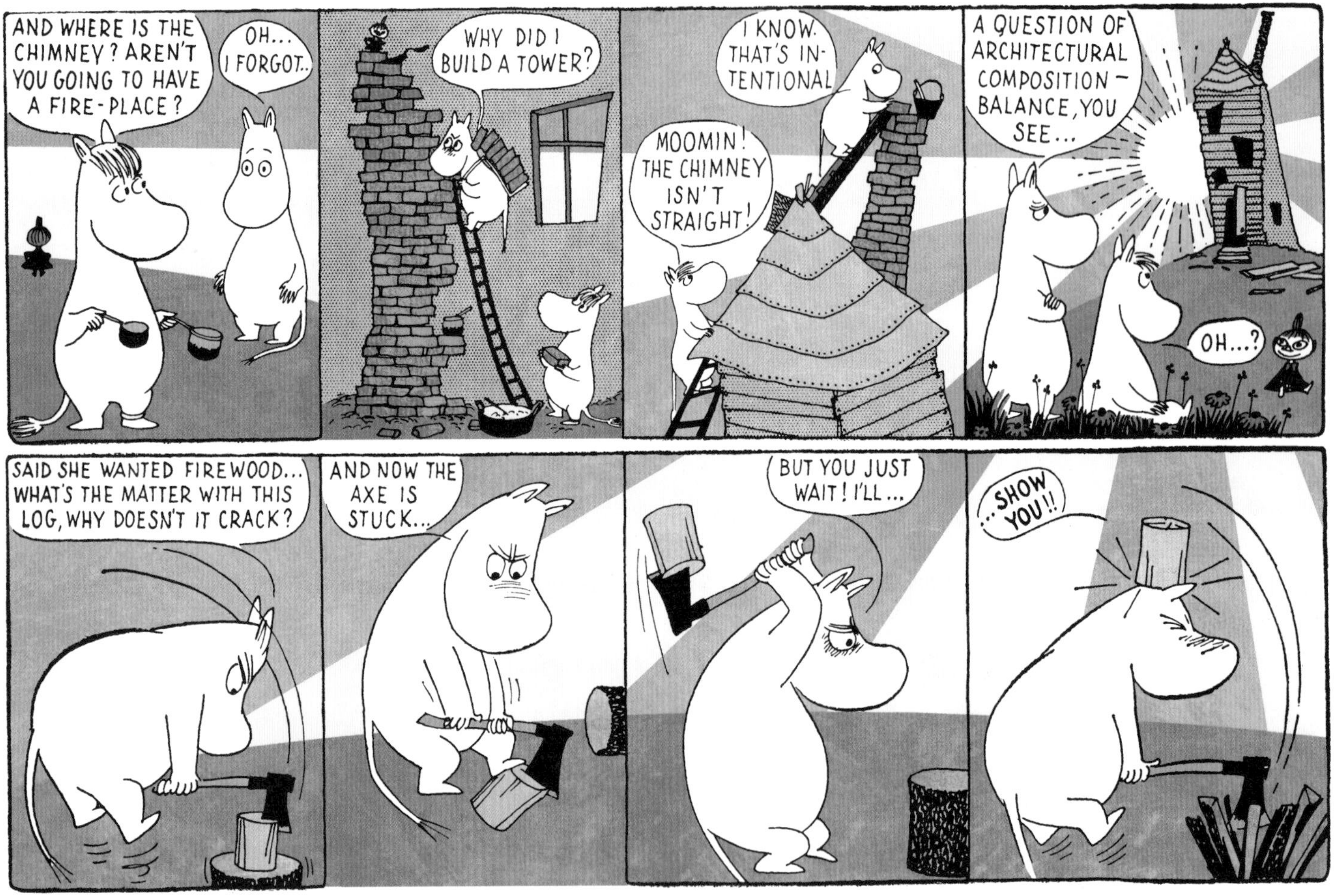
AND WHERE IS THE CHIMNEY? AREN'T YOU GOING TO HAVE A FIRE-PLACE?
OH... I FORGOT..
WHY DID I BUILD A TOWER?
MOOMIN! THE CHIMNEY ISN'T STRAIGHT!
I KNOW. THAT'S IN-TENTIONAL
A QUESTION OF ARCHITECTURAL COMPOSITION — BALANCE, YOU SEE...
OH...?
SAID SHE WANTED FIREWOOD... WHAT'S THE MATTER WITH THIS LOG, WHY DOESN'T IT CRACK?
AND NOW THE AXE IS STUCK...
BUT YOU JUST WAIT! I'LL...
...SHOW YOU!!

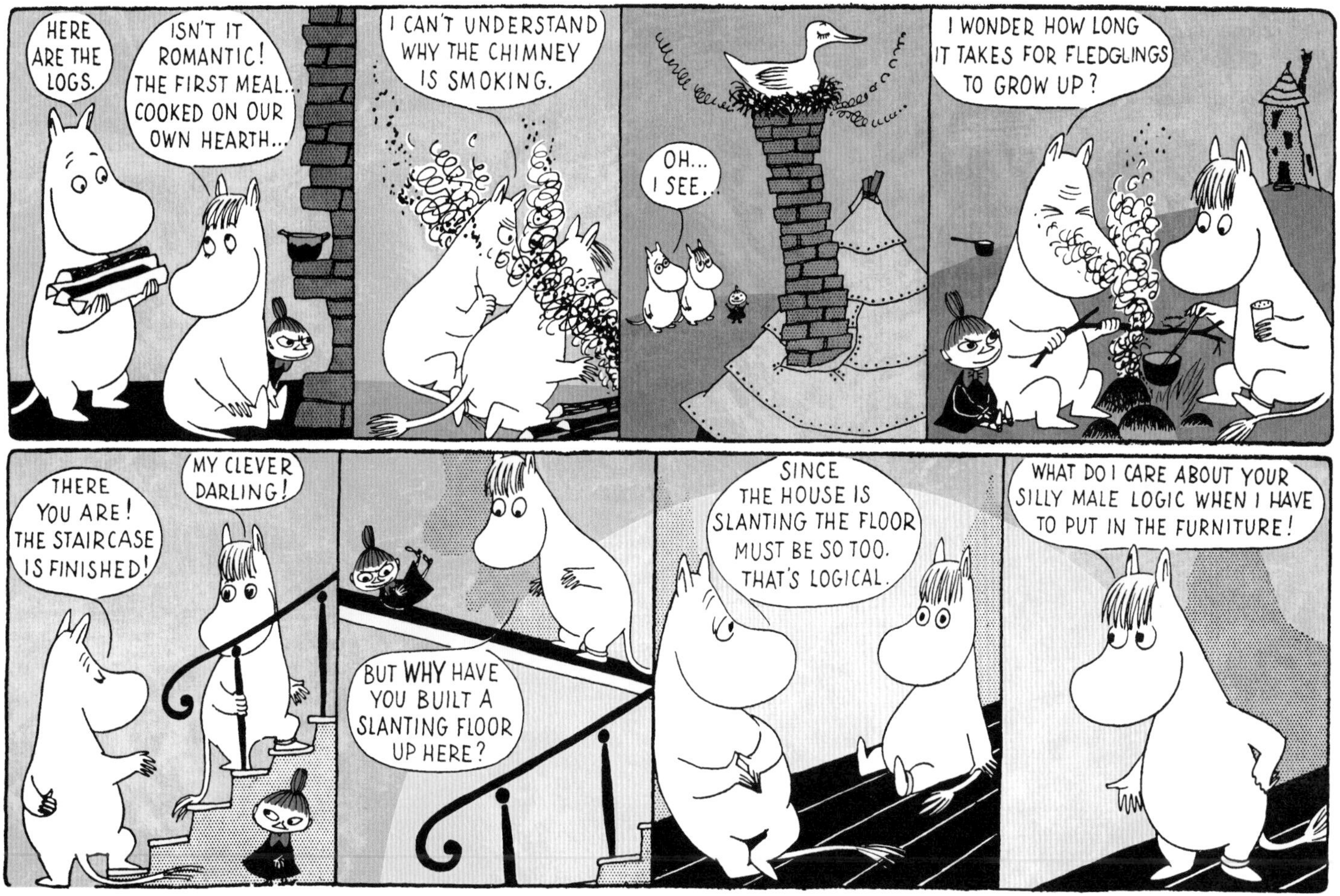
HERE ARE THE LOGS.
ISN'T IT ROMANTIC! THE FIRST MEAL... COOKED ON OUR OWN HEARTH...
I CAN'T UNDERSTAND WHY THE CHIMNEY IS SMOKING.
OH... I SEE...
I WONDER HOW LONG IT TAKES FOR FLEDGLINGS TO GROW UP?
THERE YOU ARE! THE STAIRCASE IS FINISHED!
MY CLEVER DARLING!
BUT WHY HAVE YOU BUILT A SLANTING FLOOR UP HERE?
SINCE THE HOUSE IS SLANTING THE FLOOR MUST BE SO TOO. THAT'S LOGICAL.
WHAT DO I CARE ABOUT YOUR SILLY MALE LOGIC WHEN I HAVE TO PUT IN THE FURNITURE!

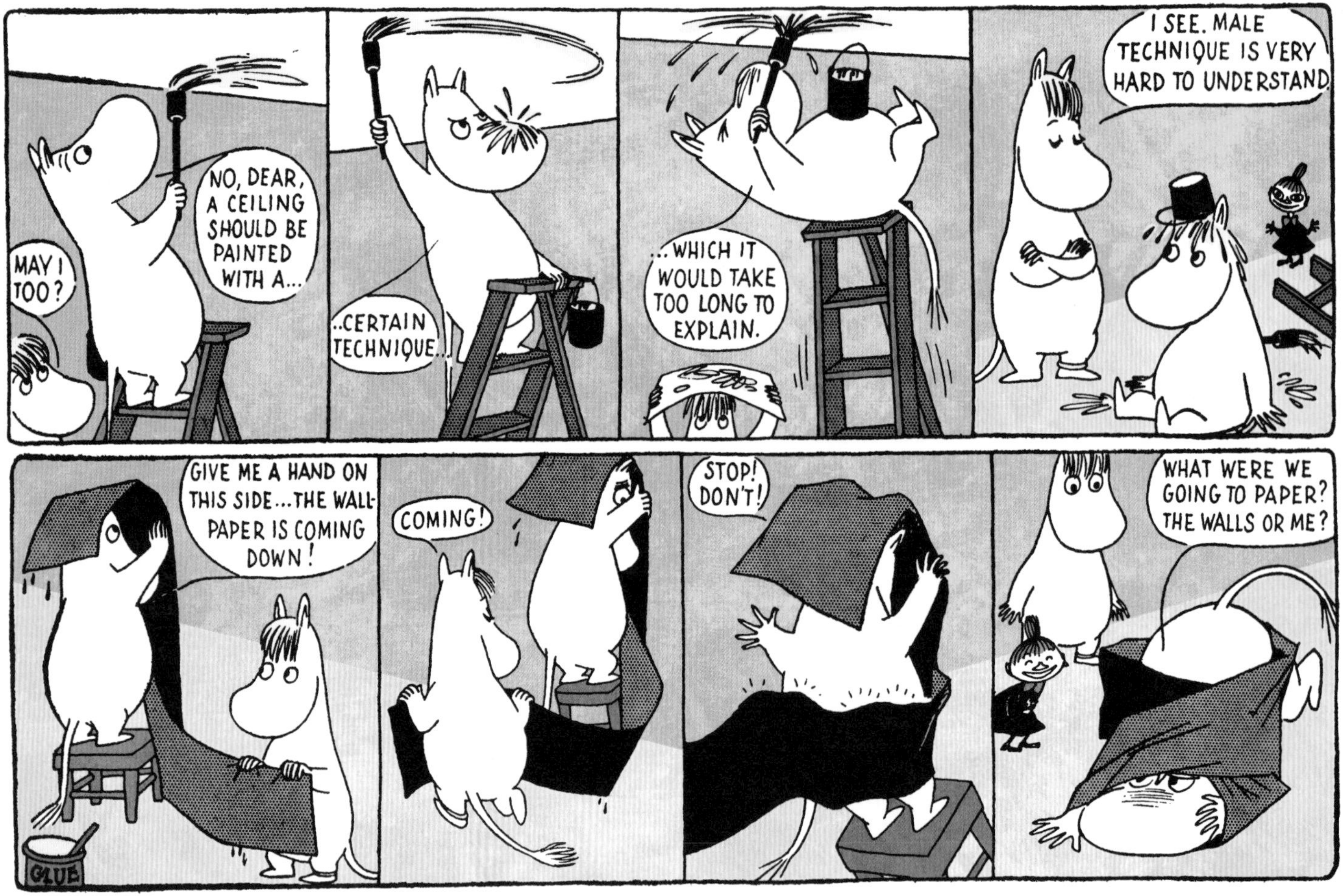
MAY I TOO?
NO, DEAR, A CEILING SHOULD BE PAINTED WITH A...
..CERTAIN TECHNIQUE...
...WHICH IT WOULD TAKE TOO LONG TO EXPLAIN.
I SEE. MALE TECHNIQUE IS VERY HARD TO UNDERSTAND.
GIVE ME A HAND ON THIS SIDE...THE WALL-PAPER IS COMING DOWN!
GLUE
COMING!
STOP! DON'T!
WHAT WERE WE GOING TO PAPER? THE WALLS OR ME?

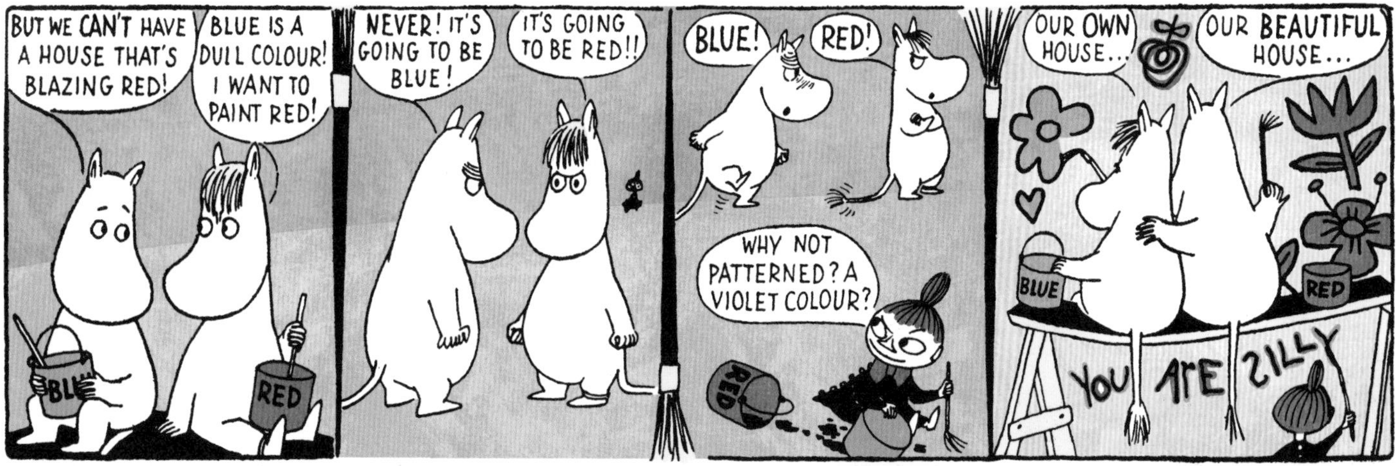
BUT WE CAN'T HAVE A HOUSE THAT'S BLAZING RED!
BLUE IS A DULL COLOUR! I WANT TO PAINT RED!
BLU
RED
NEVER! IT'S GOING TO BE BLUE!
IT'S GOING TO BE RED!!
BLUE!
RED!
WHY NOT PATTERNED? A VIOLET COLOUR?
RED
OUR OWN HOUSE...
OUR BEAUTIFUL HOUSE...
BLUE
RED
YOU ArE ƧILLY

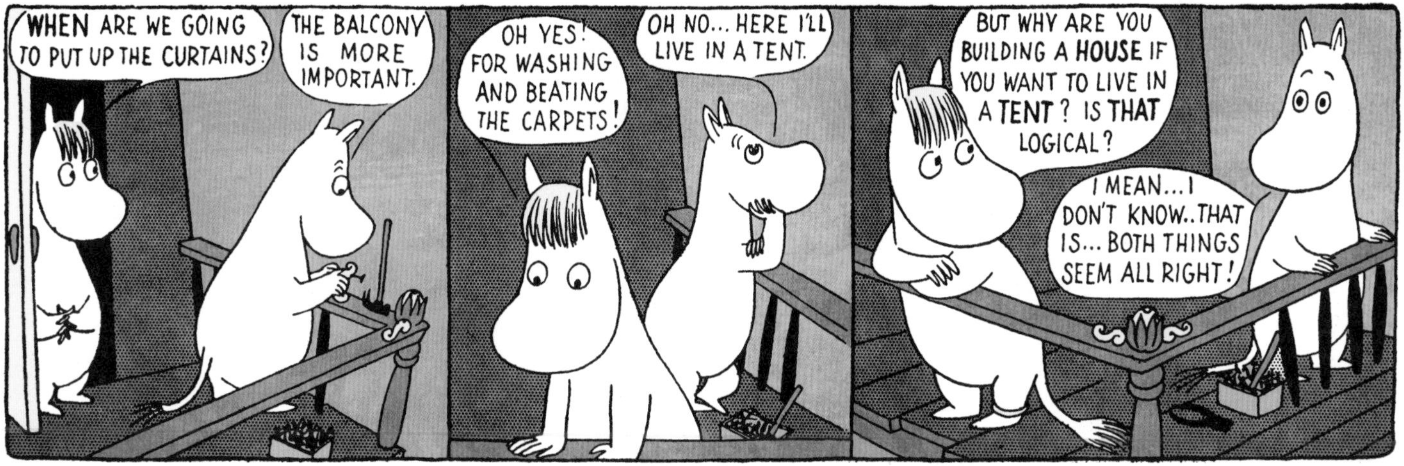
WHEN ARE WE GOING TO PUT UP THE CURTAINS?
THE BALCONY IS MORE IMPORTANT.
OH YES! FOR WASHING AND BEATING THE CARPETS!
OH NO... HERE I'LL LIVE IN A TENT.
BUT WHY ARE YOU BUILDING A HOUSE IF YOU WANT TO LIVE IN A TENT? IS THAT LOGICAL?
I MEAN... I DON'T KNOW.. THAT IS... BOTH THINGS SEEM ALL RIGHT!

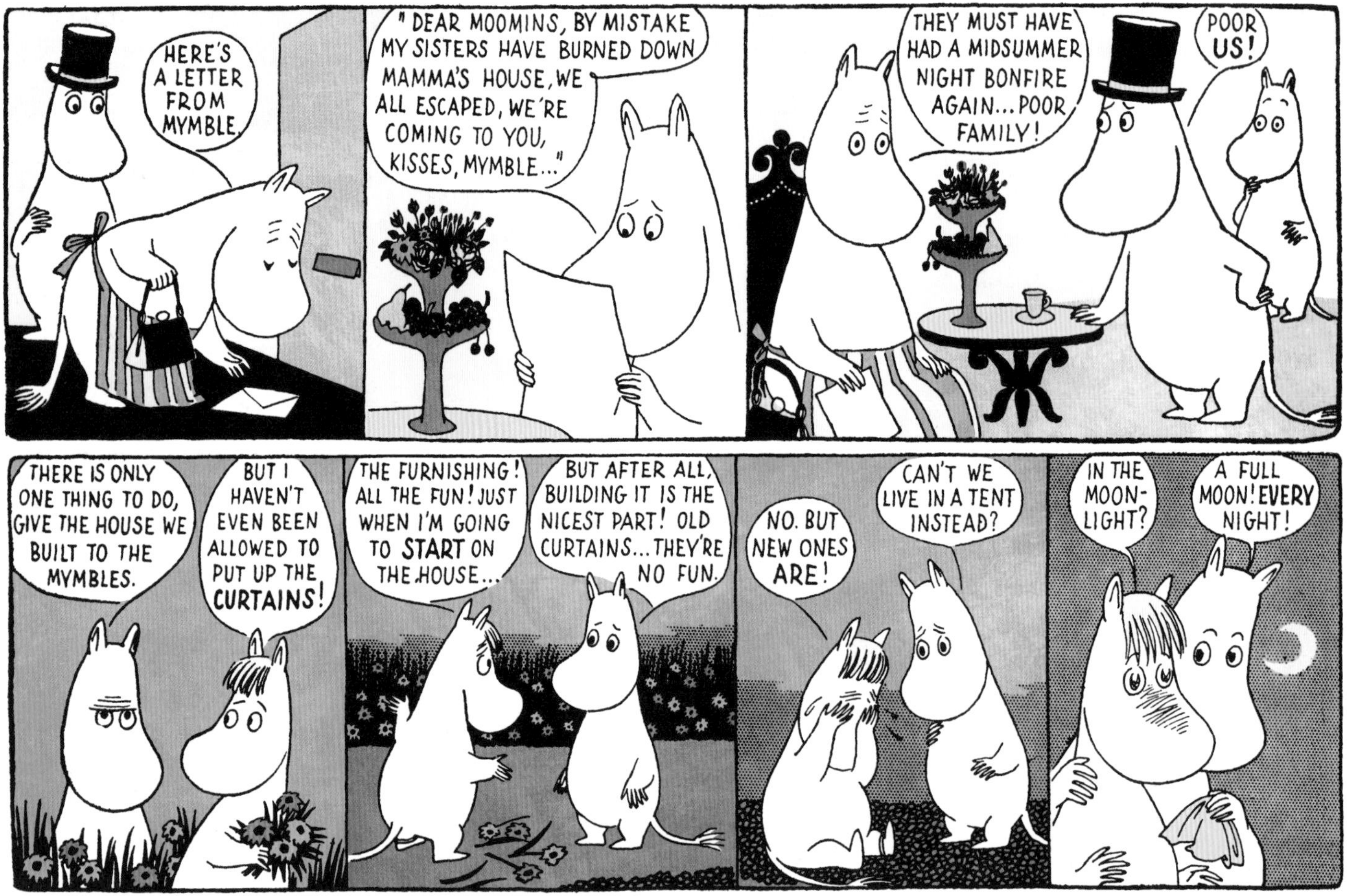
HERE'S A LETTER FROM MYMBLE.
" DEAR MOOMINS, BY MISTAKE MY SISTERS HAVE BURNED DOWN MAMMA'S HOUSE, WE ALL ESCAPED, WE'RE COMING TO YOU, KISSES, MYMBLE..."
THEY MUST HAVE HAD A MIDSUMMER NIGHT BONFIRE AGAIN... POOR FAMILY!
POOR US!
THERE IS ONLY ONE THING TO DO, GIVE THE HOUSE WE BUILT TO THE MYMBLES.
BUT I HAVEN'T EVEN BEEN ALLOWED TO PUT UP THE CURTAINS!
THE FURNISHING! ALL THE FUN! JUST WHEN I'M GOING TO START ON THE HOUSE...
BUT AFTER ALL, BUILDING IT IS THE NICEST PART! OLD CURTAINS... THEY'RE NO FUN.
NO. BUT NEW ONES ARE!
CAN'T WE LIVE IN A TENT INSTEAD?
IN THE MOON-LIGHT?
A FULL MOON! EVERY NIGHT!

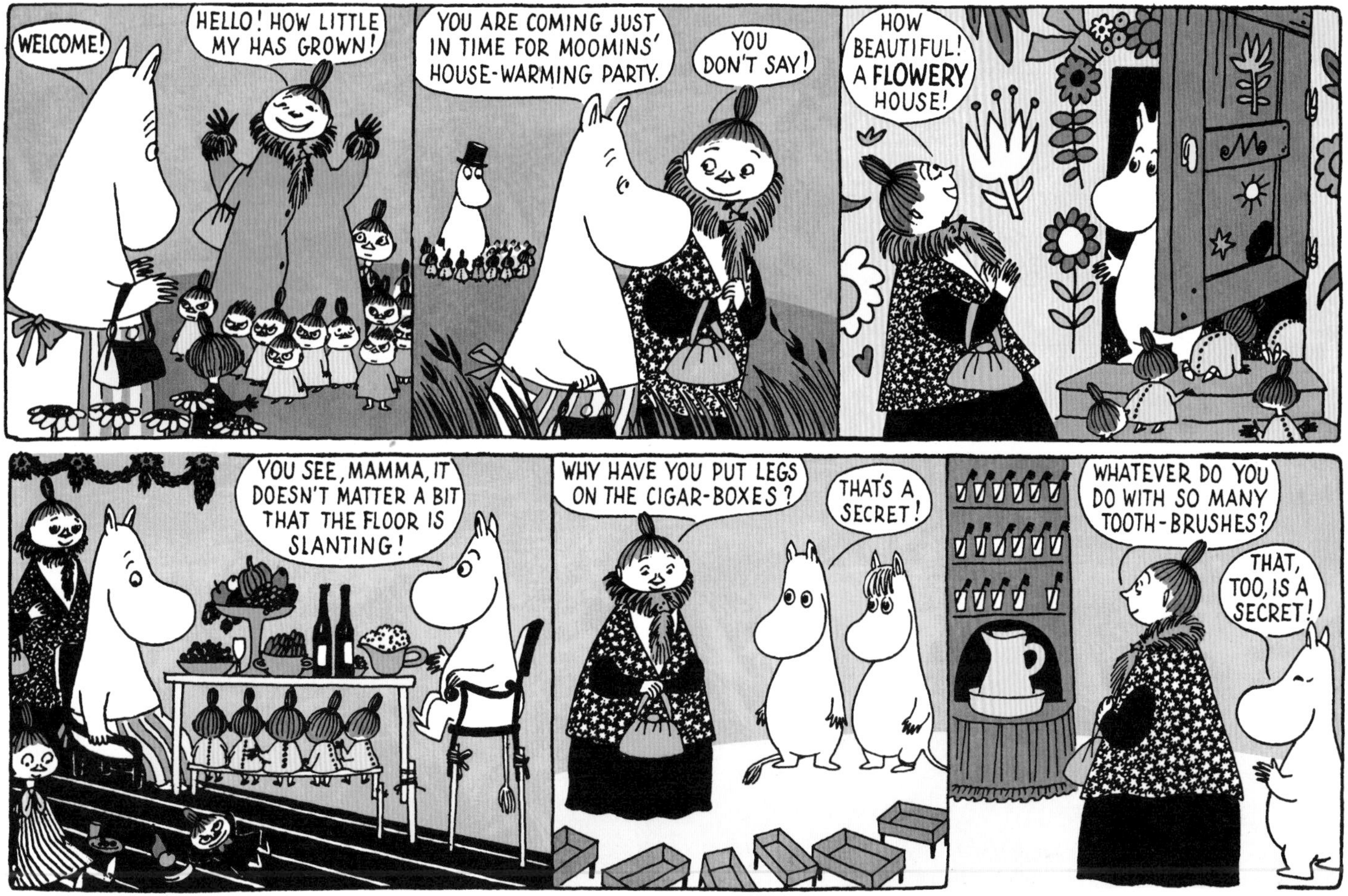

WELCOME!
HELLO! HOW LITTLE MY HAS GROWN!
YOU ARE COMING JUST IN TIME FOR MOOMINS' HOUSE-WARMING PARTY.
YOU DON'T SAY!
HOW BEAUTIFUL! A FLOWERY HOUSE!
YOU SEE, MAMMA, IT DOESN'T MATTER A BIT THAT THE FLOOR IS SLANTING!
WHY HAVE YOU PUT LEGS ON THE CIGAR-BOXES?
THAT'S A SECRET!
WHATEVER DO YOU DO WITH SO MANY TOOTH-BRUSHES?
THAT, TOO, IS A SECRET!

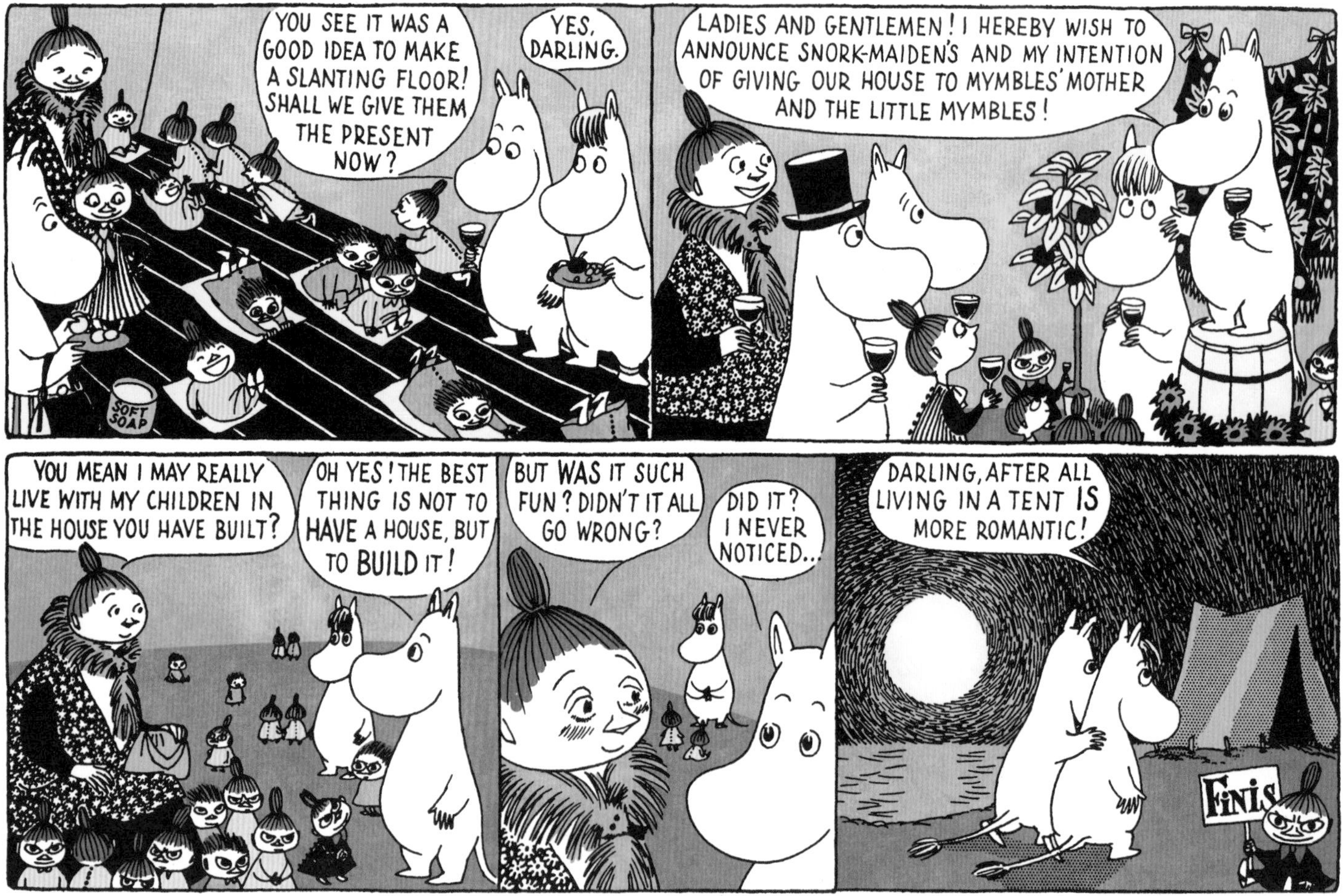

YOU SEE IT WAS A GOOD IDEA TO MAKE A SLANTING FLOOR! SHALL WE GIVE THEM THE PRESENT NOW?
YES, DARLING.
SOFT SOAP
LADIES AND GENTLEMEN! I HEREBY WISH TO ANNOUNCE SNORK-MAIDEN'S AND MY INTENTION OF GIVING OUR HOUSE TO MYMBLES' MOTHER AND THE LITTLE MYMBLES!
YOU MEAN I MAY REALLY LIVE WITH MY CHILDREN IN THE HOUSE YOU HAVE BUILT?
OH YES! THE BEST THING IS NOT TO HAVE A HOUSE, BUT TO BUILD IT!
BUT WAS IT SUCH FUN? DIDN'T IT ALL GO WRONG?
DID IT? I NEVER NOTICED...
DARLING, AFTER ALL LIVING IN A TENT IS MORE ROMANTIC!
FINIS

Let Enfant take you away to the exciting world of
MOOMINVALLEY! NOW IN FULL COLOR!

Moomin Falls in Love
Moominvalley Turns Jungle
Moomin's Winter Follies

AVAILABLE NOW!

Moomin and the Sea
Moomin and the Comet

COMING SPRING 2013

Available at finer comics shops and bookstores
everywhere, or from drawnandquarterly.com

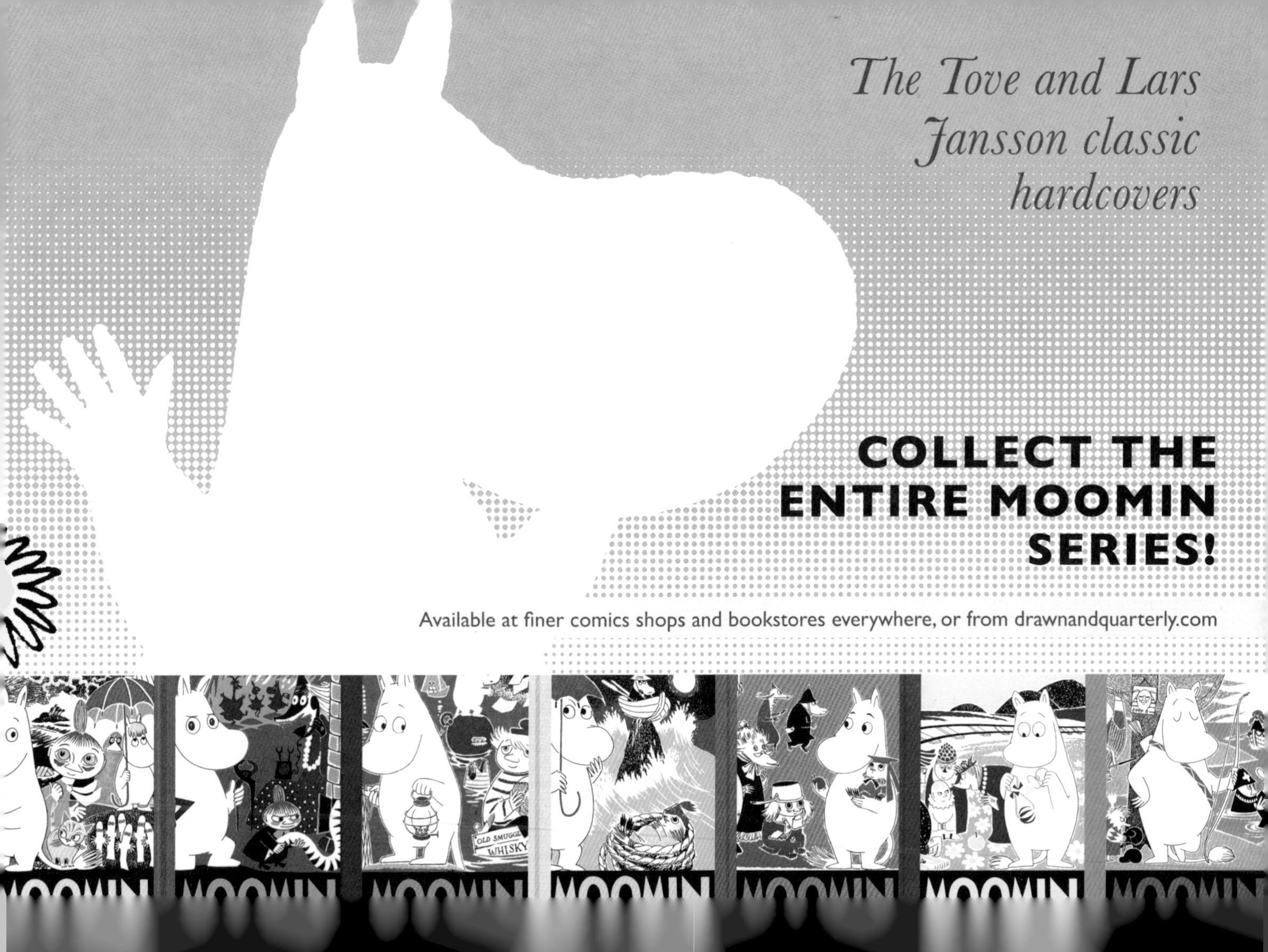

The Tove and Lars Jansson classic hardcovers
COLLECT THE ENTIRE MOOMIN SERIES!
Available at finer comics shops and bookstores everywhere, or from drawnandquarterly.com

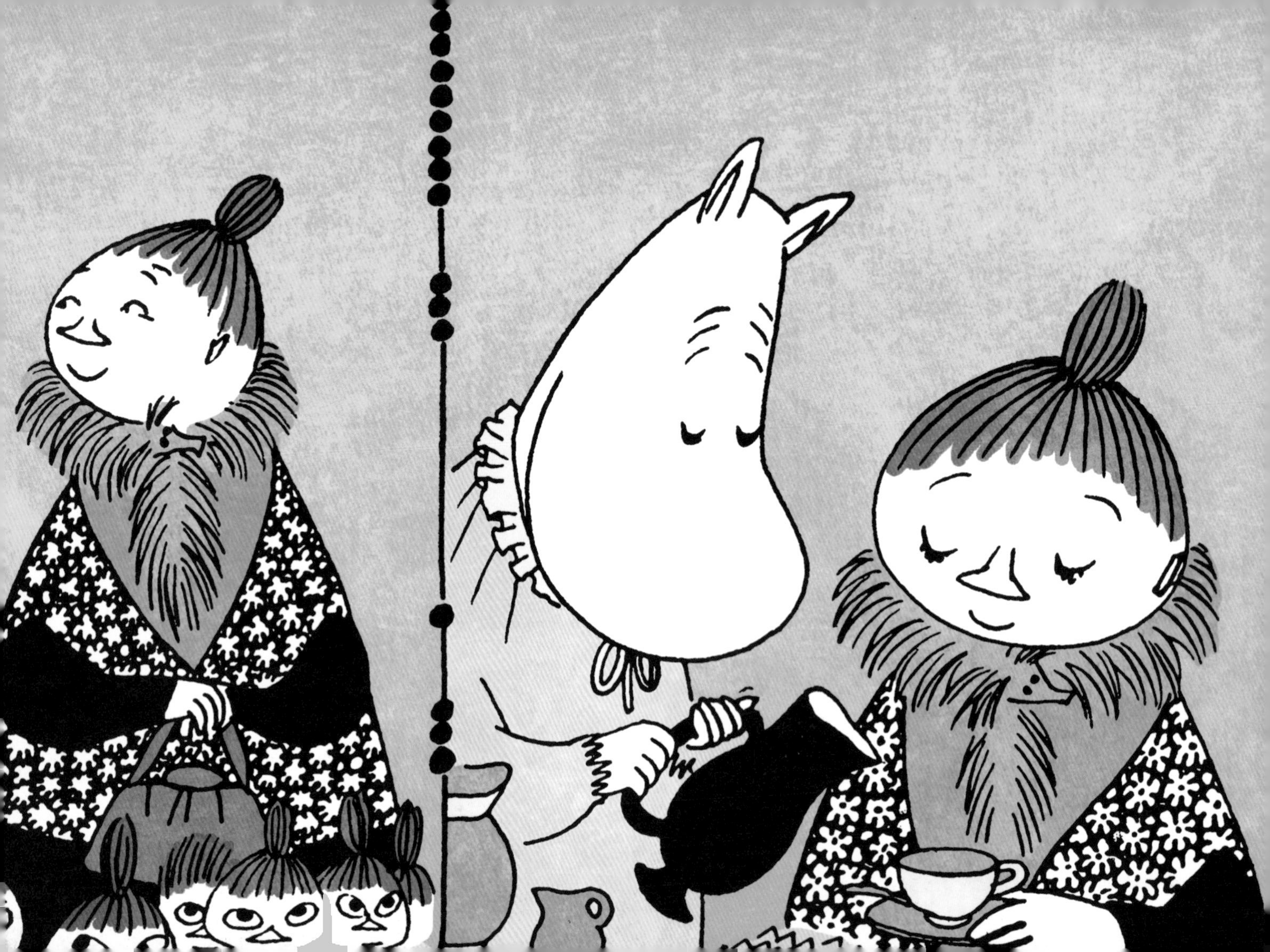

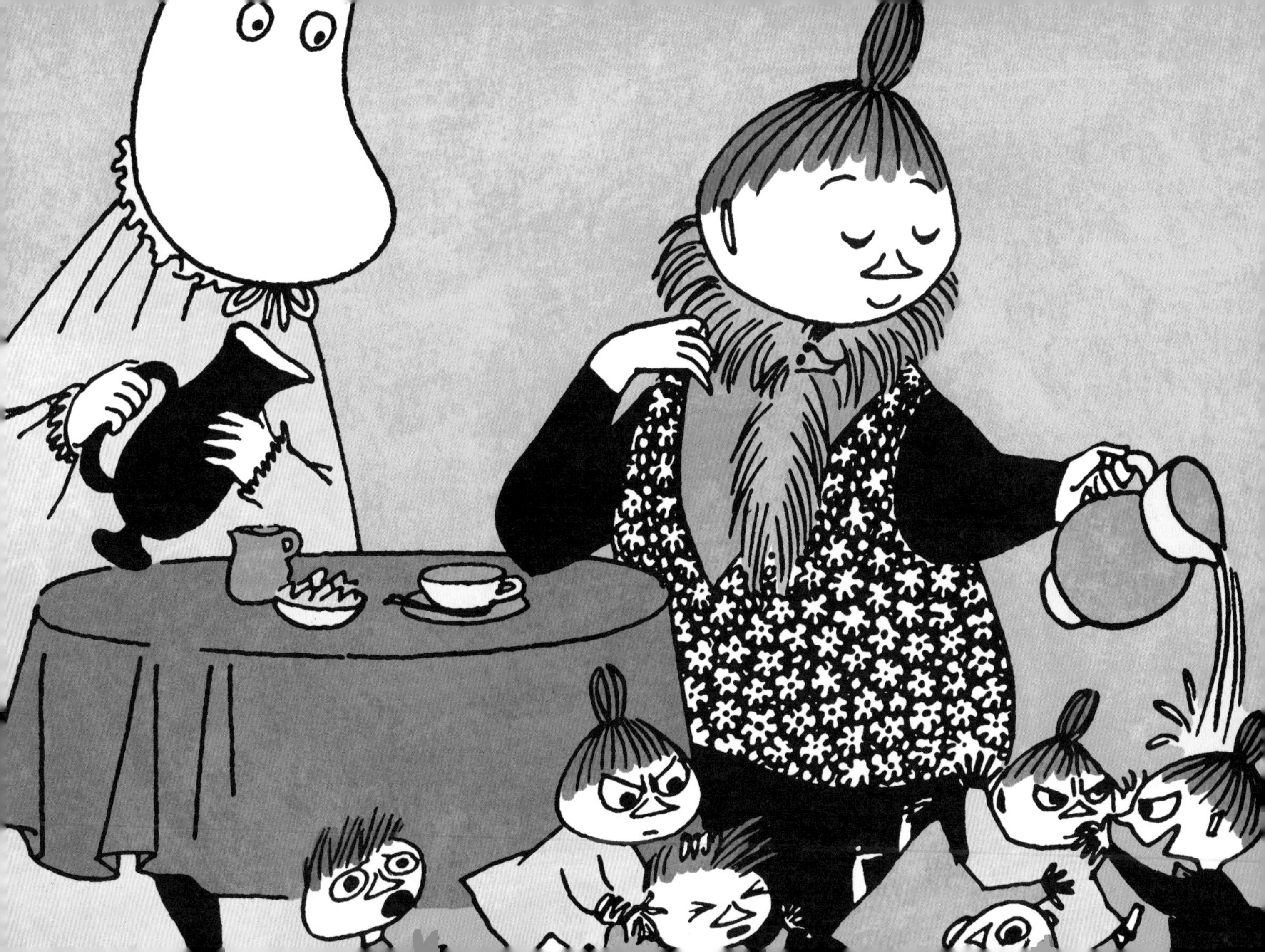

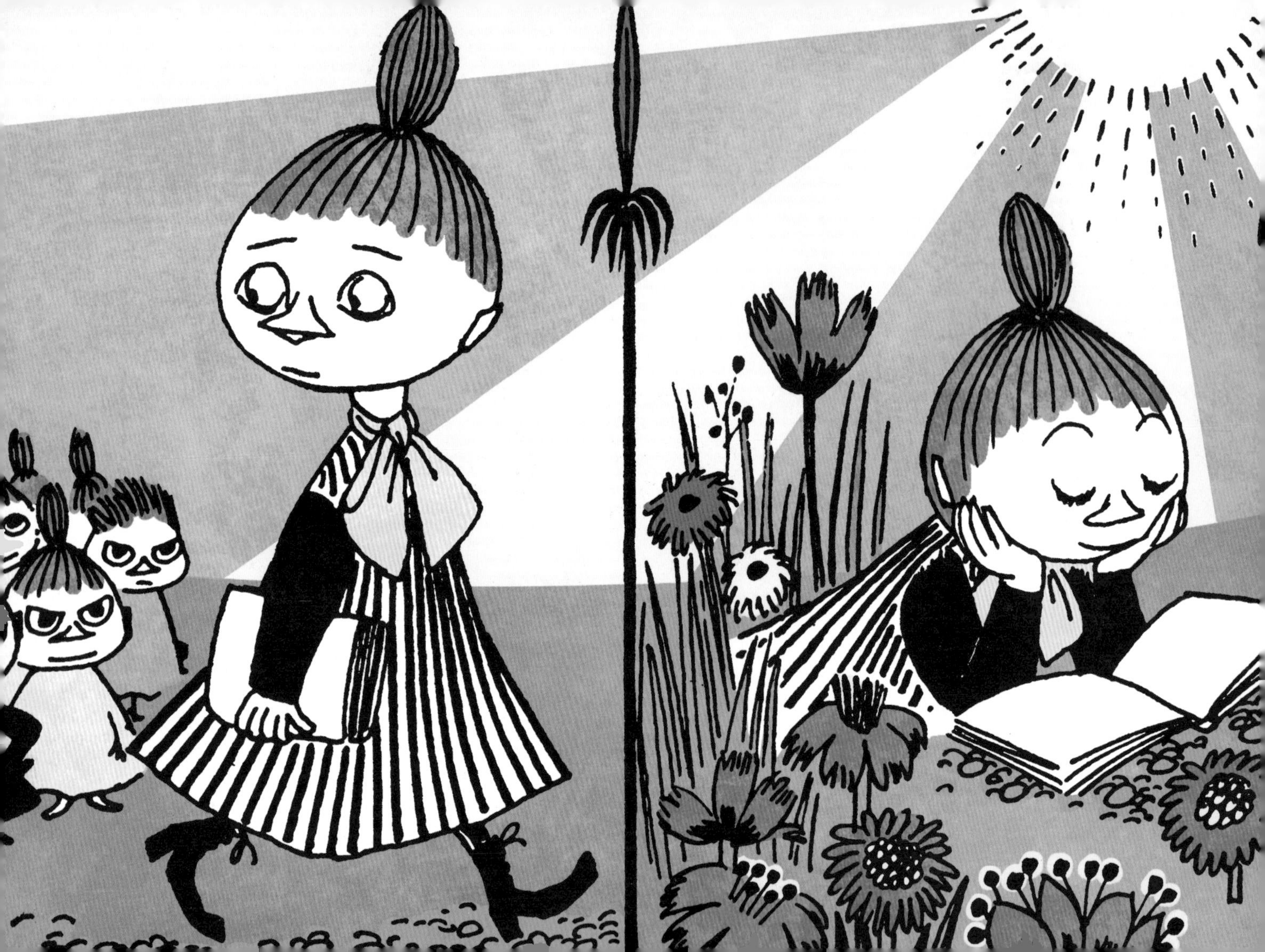

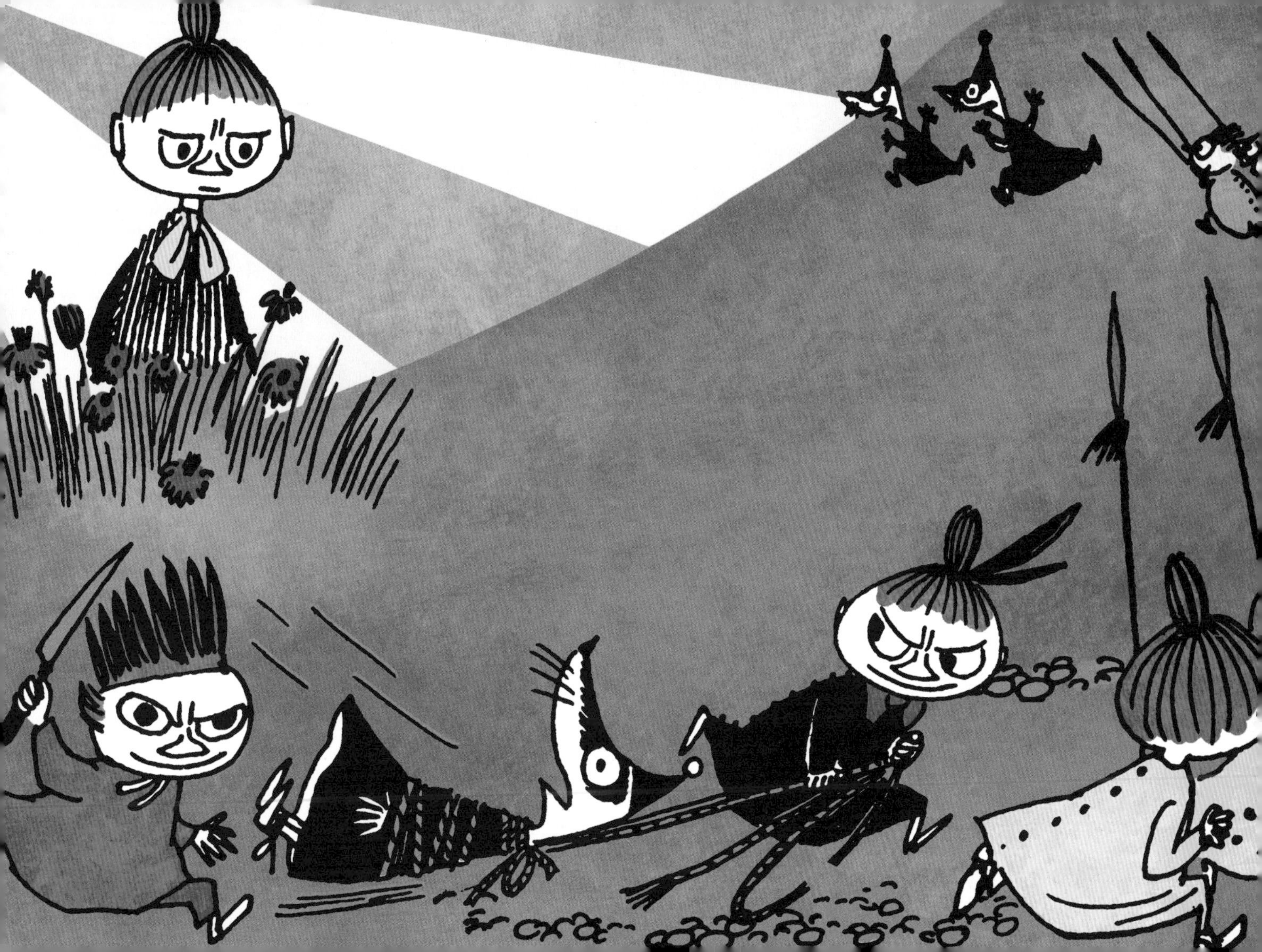

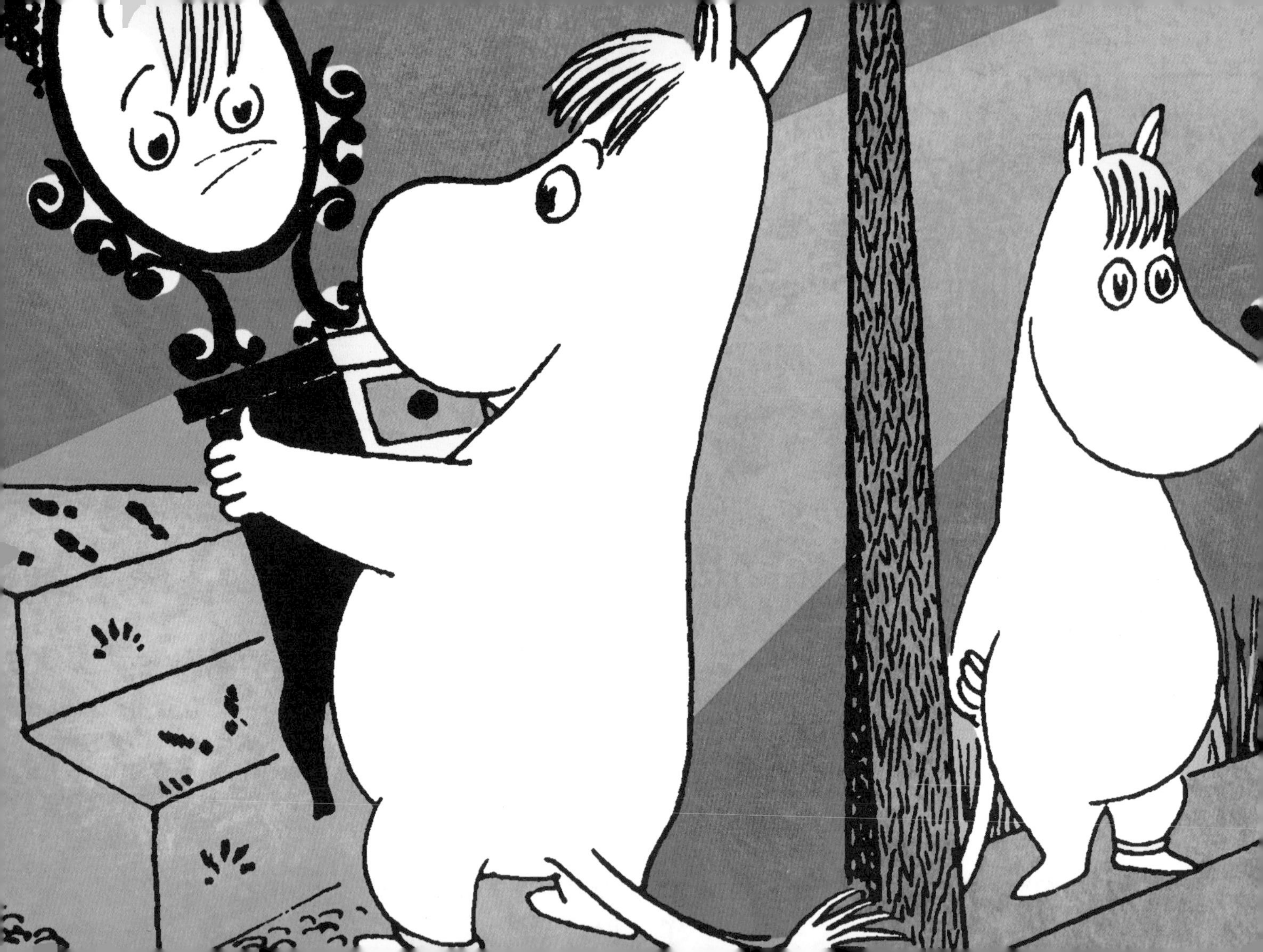